Kabuliwala and other stories

Rabindranath Tagore

maple press

Published by

MAPLE PRESS PRIVATE LIMITED
office: A-63, Sector 58, Noida 201301, U.P., India
phone: +91 120 455 3581, 455 3583
email: info@maplepress.co.in
website: www.maplepress.co.in

Reprint 2021 in India

ISBN: 978-93-89225-23-5

Contents

1
The Kabuliwala

My five years old daughter Mini cannot live without chattering. I really believe that in all her life she has not wasted a minute in silence. Her mother is often vexed at this, and would stop her prattle, but I would not. To see Mini quiet, is unnatural and I cannot bear it long. And so my own talk with her is always lively.

One morning, for instance, when I was in the midst of the seventeenth chapter of my new novel, my little Mini stole into the room, and putting her hand into mine and said, "Father! Ramdayal, the door-keeper calls a crow, 'a krow!' He doesn't know anything, does he?"

Before I could explain to her the differences of language in this world, she was embarked on the full tide of another subject. "What do you think, Father? Bhola says there is an elephant in the clouds, blowing water out of his trunk, and that is why it rains!"

And then, darting off anew, while I sat still making ready some reply to this last saying, "Father! What relation is mother to you?"

"My dear little sister-in-law!" I murmured involuntarily to myself, but with a grave face contrived to answer, "Go and play with Bhola, Mini! I am busy!"

The window of my room overlooks the road. The child had seated herself at my feet near my table, and was playing softly, drumming on her knees. I was hard at work on my seventeenth chapter, where Protap Singh, the hero, had just caught Kanchanlata, the heroine, in his arms, and was about to escape with her by the third story window of the castle, when all of a sudden Mini left her play, and ran to the window, crying, "A Kabuliwala! A Kabuliwala!" Sure enough in the street below was a kabuliwala, passing slowly along. He wore the loose soiled clothing of his people, with a tall turban, there was a bag on his back, and he carried boxes of grapes in his hand.

I couldn't tell what my daughter felt at the sight of this man, but she began to call him loudly. "Ah!" I thought, "He will come in, and my seventeenth chapter will never be finished!" At which exact moment the kabuliwala turned, and looked up at the child. When she saw this, overcome by terror, she fled to her mother's protection, and disappeared. She had a blind belief that inside the bag, which the big man carried, there were perhaps two or three other children like her. The pedlar meanwhile entered my doorway, and greeted me with a smiling face.

So precarious was the position of my hero and my heroine that my first impulse was to stop and buy something, since the man had been called. I made some small purchases, and a conversation began about Abdurrahman, the Russians, the English, and the Frontier Policy.

As he was about to leave when he asked, "And where is the little girl, sir?"

And I, thinking that Mini must get rid of her false fear, had her brought out.

She stood by my chair, and looked at the kabuliwala and his bag. He offered her nuts and raisins, but she would not be tempted, and only clung closer to me, with all her doubts increased.

This was their first meeting.

One morning, however, not many days later, as I was leaving the house, I was startled to find Mini, seated on a bench near the door, laughing and talking, with the great kabuliwala at her feet.

In all her life, it appeared like my small daughter had never found so patient a listener, except her father. And already the corner of her little sari was stuffed with almonds and raisins, the gift of her visitor, "Why did you give her those?" I said, and taking out an eight-bit, I handed it to him. The man accepted the money without demur, and slipped it into his pocket.

Alas, on my return an hour later, I found the unfortunate coin had made twice its own worth of trouble! For the kabuliwala had given it to Mini, and her mother catching sight of the bright round object, had pounced on the child with, "Where did you get that eight-*anna* bit?"

"The Kabuliwala gave it to me," said Mini cheerfully.

"The Kabuliwala gave it you!" cried her mother much shocked, "Oh, Mini! How could you take it from him?"

Entering at the moment, I saved her from impending disaster, and proceeded to make my own inquiries.

It was not the first or second time, I found, that the two had met. The kabuliwala had overcome the child's first terror by a judicious bribery of nuts and almonds, and the two were now great friends.

They had many quaint jokes, which afforded them much amusement. Seated in front of him, looking down on his gigantic frame in all her tiny dignity, Mini would ripple her face with laughter, and begin, "O Kabuliwala, Kabuliwala, what have you got in your bag?"

And he would reply, in the nasal accents of the mountaineer, "An elephant!" Not much cause for merriment, perhaps, but how they both enjoyed the witticism! And for me, this child's talk with a grown-up man had always in it something strangely fascinating.

Then, the kabuliwala would take his turn, "Well, little one, when are you going to the father-in-law's house?"

Now most small Bengali maidens have heard long ago about the father-in-law's house, but we, being a little new-fangled, had kept these things from our child, and Mini at this question must have been a trifle bewildered. But she would not show it, and with ready tact replied, "Are you going there?"

Amongst men of the kabuliwala's class, however, it is well known that the words father-in-law's house have a double meaning. It is a euphemism for jail, the place where we are well cared for, at no expense to ourselves. The sturdy pedlar would take my daughter's question in this sense. "Ah!" he would say, shaking his fist at an invisible policeman, "I will thrash my father-in-law!" Hearing this, and picturing the poor discomfited relative, Mini would go off into peals of laughter, in which her formidable friend would join.

These were autumn mornings, the very time of year when kings of old went forth to conquest, and I, never stirring from my little corner in Calcutta, would let my mind wander over the whole world. At the very name of another country, my heart would go out to it, and at the sight of a foreigner in the streets, I would fall to weaving a network of dreams – the mountains, the glens, and the forests of his distant home, with his cottage in its setting, and the free and independent life of faraway wilds. Perhaps the scenes of travel conjure themselves up before me, and pass and repass in my imagination all the more vividly, because I lead such a vegetable existence, that a call to travel would fall upon me like a thunderbolt. In the presence of this kabuliwala, I was immediately transported to the foot of arid mountain peaks, with narrow little defiles twisting in and out amongst their towering heights. I could see the string of camels bearing the merchandise, and the company of turbaned merchants, carrying some of their queer old firearms, and some of their spears, journeying downward towards the plains.

I could see – but at some such point Mini's mother would intervene, imploring me to be "beware of that man."

Mini's mother is unfortunately a very timid lady. Whenever she hears a noise in the street, or sees people coming towards the house, she always jumps to the conclusion that they are either thieves, or drunkards, or snakes, or tigers, or malaria or cockroaches, or caterpillars, or an English sailor. Even after all these years of experience, she is not able to overcome her terror. So she was full of doubts about the kabuliwala, and used to beg me to keep a watchful eye on him.

I tried to laugh her fear gently away, but then she would turn round on me seriously, and ask me solemn questions.

Were children never kidnapped?

Was it, then, not true that there was slavery in Kabul?

Was it so very absurd that this big man should be able to carry off a tiny child?

I urged that, though not impossible, it was highly improbable. But this was not enough, and her dread persisted. As it was indefinite, however, it did not seem right to forbid the man at the house and the intimacy went unchecked.

Once a year in the middle of January, Rahmun, the kabuliwala was in the habit of returning to his country, and as the time approached he would be very busy, going from house to house collecting his debts. This year, however, he could always find time to come and see Mini. It would have seemed to an outsider that there was some conspiracy between the two, for when he could not come in the morning, he would appear in the evening.

Even to me it was a little startling now and then, in the corner of a dark room, suddenly to surprise this tall, loose-garmented, much bebagged man, but when Mini would run in smiling, with her, "O! Kabuliwala! Kabuliwala!" and the two friends, so far apart in age, would subside into their old laughter and their old jokes. I felt reassured.

One morning, a few days before he had made up his mind to go, I was correcting my proof sheets in my study. It was chilly weather. Through the window the rays of the sun touched my feet, and the slight warmth was very welcome. It was almost eight o' clock, and the early pedestrians were returning home, with their heads covered. All at once, I heard uproar in the street, and looking out, saw Rahmun being led away bound between two policemen, and behind them a crowd of curious boys. There were blood-stains on the clothes of the kabuliwala, and one of the policemen carried a knife. Hurrying out, I stopped them, and enquired what it all meant. Partly from one, partly from another, I gathered that a certain neighbour had owed the pedlar something for a Rampuri shawl, but had falsely denied having bought it, and that in the course of the quarrel, Rahmun had struck him. Now in the heat of his excitement, the prisoner began calling his enemy all sorts of names, when suddenly in a verandah of my house appeared my little Mini, with her usual exclamation, "O Kabuliwala! Kabuliwala!" Rahmun's face lighted up as he turned to her. He had no bag under his arm today, so she could not discuss the elephant with him. She proceeded to the next question, "Are you going to the father-in-law's house?" Rahmun laughed and said, "Just where I am going, little one!" Then seeing that the reply did not amuse the child, he held up his fettered hands. "Ali," he said, "I would have thrashed that old father-in-law, but my hands are bound!"

On a charge of murderous assault, Rahmun was sentenced to some years of imprisonment.

Time passed away, and he was forgotten. The accustomed work in the accustomed place was ours, and the thought of the once-free mountaineer spending his years in prison seldom or never occurred to us. Even my light-hearted Mini, I am ashamed to say, forgot her old friend. New companions filled her life. As she grew older, she spent more of her time with girls. So much time indeed did she spend with them that she came no more, as she used to do, to her father's room. I was scarcely on speaking terms with her.

Years passed away. It was once more the autumn season and we had made arrangements for our Mini's marriage. It was to take place during the puja holidays. With Durga returning to Kailas, the light of our home also was to depart to her husband's house, and leave her father's in the shadow.

The morning was bright. After the rains, there was a sense of ablution in the air, and the sun-rays looked like pure gold. So bright were they that they gave a beautiful radiance even to the sordid brick walls of our Calcutta lanes. Since dawn, the wedding-pipes had been sounding, and at each beat my own heart throbbed. The wail of the tune, Bhairavi, seemed to intensify my pain at the approaching separation. My Mini was to be married tonight.

In the courtyard the canopy had to be slung on its bamboo poles, the chandeliers with their tinkling sound must be hung in each room and verandah. There was no end of hurry and excitement. I was sitting in my study, looking through the accounts, when some one entered, saluting respectfully, and stood before me. It was Rahmun, the kabuliwala. At first, I did not recognise him. He had no bag, nor the long hair, nor the same vigour that he used to have. But he smiled, and I knew it was my Mini's favourite kabuliwala.

"When did you come, Rahmun?" I asked him.

"Last evening," he said, "I was released from jail."

The words struck harsh upon my ears. I had never before talked with one who had wounded his fellow, and my heart shrank within itself, when I realised this, for I felt that the day would have been better-omened had he not turned up.

"There are ceremonies going on," I said, "and I am busy. Could you perhaps come another day?"

At once he turned to go, but as he reached the door he hesitated, and said, "May I not see the little one, sir, for a moment?" It was his belief that Mini was still the same. He had pictured her running to him as she used, calling "O Kabuliwala! Kabuliwala!" He had imagined too that they would laugh and talk together, just as of old. In fact, in memory of former days he had brought, carefully wrapped up in paper, a few almonds and raisins and grapes, obtained somehow from a countryman, for his own little fund was dispersed.

I said again, "There is a ceremony in the house, and you will not be able to see anyone today."

The man's face fell. He looked wistfully at me for a moment, said, "Good morning" and went out. I felt sorry and would have called him back, but I found him returning of his own accord. He came close up to me holding out his offerings and said, "I brought these few things, sir, for the little one. Will you give them to her?"

I took them and was going to pay him, but he caught my hand and said, "You are very kind, sir! Keep me in your memories. Do not offer me money! You have a little girl, I too have one like her in my own home. I think of her, and bring fruits to your child, not to make a profit for myself."

Saying this, he put his hand inside his big loose robe, and brought out a small and dirty piece of paper. With great care he unfolded this, and smoothed it out with both hands on my table. It bore the impression of a little hand. Not a photograph. Not a drawing. But an impression of an ink-smeared hand laid flat on the paper. This touch of his own little daughter had been always on his heart, as he had come year after year to Calcutta, to sell his wares in the streets.

Tears came to my eyes. I forgot that he was a poor Kabuli fruit-seller, while I was – but no, what was I more than him? He was also a father. That impression of the hand of his little Parbati in her distant mountain home reminded me of my own little Mini.

I sent for Mini immediately from the inner apartment. Many difficulties were raised, but I would not listen. Clad in the red silk of her wedding day, with the sandal paste on her forehead, and adorned as a young bride, Mini came, and stood bashfully before me.

The kabuliwala looked a little staggered at the apparition. He could not revive their old friendship. At last he smiled and said, "Little one, are you going to your father-in-law's house?"

But Mini now understood the meaning of the word "father-in-law" and she could not answer as she used to. She flushed up at the question, and stood before him with her bride-like face turned down.

I remembered the day when the kabuliwala and my Mini had first met, and I felt sad. When she had gone, Rahmun heaved a deep sigh, and sat down on the floor. The idea had suddenly come to him that his daughter too must have grown in this long time, and that he would have to make friends with her anew. Assuredly he would not find her, as he used to know her. And besides, what might not have happened to her in these eight years?

The marriage-pipes sounded, and the mild autumn sun streamed round us. But Rahmun sat in the little Calcutta lane, and saw before him the barren mountains of Afghanistan.

I took out a bank-note, and gave it to him, saying, "Go back to your own daughter, Rahmun, in your own country, and may the happiness of your meeting bring good fortune to my child!"

Having made this present, I had to curtail some of the festivities. I could not have the electric lights I had intended, or the military band, and the ladies of the house were despondent at it. But to me the wedding feast was all the brighter for the thought that in a distant land a long-lost father met again with his only child.

2
The Victory

Princess Ajita was her name. The court poet of King Narayan had never seen her. On the day, he recited a new poem to the king he raised his voice so that his pitch which could be heard by unseen hearers in the screened balcony high above the hall. He sent up his song towards the star-land out of his reach, where, circled with light, the planet who ruled his destiny shone unknown and out of ken.

He would espy some shadow moving behind the veil. A tinkling sound would come to his car from afar, and would set him dreaming of the ankles whose tiny golden bells sang at each step. Ah, the rosy red tender feet that walked the dust of the earth like God's mercy on the fallen! The poet had placed them on the altar of his heart, where he wove his songs to the tune of those golden bells. Doubt never arose in his mind as to whose shadow it was that moved behind the screen, and whose anklets they were that sang to the time of his beating heart.

Manjari, the maid of the princess, passed by the poet's house on her way to the river, and she never missed a day to have a few words with him on the sly. When she found the road deserted, and the shadow of dusk on the land, she would boldly enter his room, and sit at the corner of his carpet. There was a suspicion of an added care in the choice of the colour of her veil, in the setting of the flower in her hair.

People smiled and whispered at this, and they were not to blame. For Shekhar, the poet never took the trouble to hide the fact that these meetings were a pure joy to him.

The meaning of her name was the spray of flowers. One must confess that for an ordinary mortal it was sufficient in its sweetness. But Shekhar made his own addition to this name, and called her the 'Spray of Spring Flowers'. And ordinary mortals shook their heads and said, "Ah, me!"

In the spring songs, the poet sang the praise of the spray of spring flowers was conspicuously reiterated, and the king winked and smiled at him when he heard it, and the poet smiled in answer.

The king would put him the question, "Is it the business of the bee merely to hum in the court of the spring?"

The poet would answer, "No, but also to sip the honey of the spray of spring flowers."

And they all laughed in the king's hall. And it was rumoured that Princess Ajita also laughed at her maid's accepting the poet's name for her, and Manjari felt glad in her heart.

Thus, truth and falsehood mingle in life – and to what God builds man adds his own decoration.

Only those were pure truths which were sung by the poet. The theme was Krishna, the lover god, and Radha, the beloved, the Eternal Man and the Eternal Woman, the sorrow that comes from the beginning of time, and the joy without end. The truth of these songs was tested in his inmost heart by everybody from the beggar to the king himself. The poet's songs were on the lips of all. At the merest glimmer of the moon and the faintest whisper of the summer breeze his songs would break forth in the land from windows and courtyards, from sailing-boats, from shadows of the wayside trees, in innumerable voices.

Thus, passed the days happily. The poet recited, the king listened, the hearers applauded, Manjari passed and repassed by the poet's room on her way to the river, the shadow flitted behind the screened balcony, and the tiny golden bells tinkled from afar.

Just then set forth from his home in the south a poet on his path of conquest. He came to King Narayan, in the kingdom of Amarapur. He stood before the throne, and uttered a verse in praise of the king. He had challenged all the court poets on his way, and his career of victory had been unbroken.

The king received him with honour, and said, "Poet, I wholeheartedly welcome you."

Pundarik, the poet, proudly replied, "Sire, I ask for war."

Shekhar, the court poet of the king did not know how the battle of the muse was to be waged. He couldn't sleep at night. The mighty figure of the famous Pundarik, his sharp nose curved like a scimitar, and his proud head tilted on one side, haunted the poet's vision in the dark.

Shekhar entered the arena in the morning with a trembling heart. The theatre was filled with the crowd.

The poet greeted his rival with a smile and a bow. Pundarik returned it with a slight toss of his head, and turned his face towards his circle of adoring followers with a smile. Shekhar cast his glance towards the screened balcony high above, and saluted his lady in his mind, saying, "If I am the winner at the combat today, my lady, thy victorious name shall be glorified."

The trumpet sounded. The great crowd stood up, shouting victory to the king. The king, dressed in an ample robe of white, slowly came into the hall like a floating cloud of autumn, and sat on his throne.

Pundarik stood up, and the vast hall became still. With his head raised high and chest expanded, he began in his thundering voice to recite the praise of King Narayan. His words burst upon the walls of the hall like breakers of the sea, and seemed to rattle against the ribs of the listening crowd. The skill with which he gave varied meanings to the name Narayan, and wove each letter of it through the web of his verses in all mariner of combinations, took away the breath of his amazed hearers.

For some minutes after he took his seat his voice continued to vibrate among the numberless pillars of the king's court and in thousands of speechless hearts. The learned professors who had come from distant lands raised their right hands, and cried, "Bravo!"

The king threw a glance on Shekhar's face, and Shekhar in answer raised for a moment his eyes full of pain towards his master, and then stood up like a stricken deer at bay. His face was pale, his bashfulness was almost that of a woman, his slight youthful figure, delicate in its outline, seemed like a tensely strung vina ready to break out in music at the least touch.

His head was bent, his voice was low, when he began. The first few verses were almost inaudible. Then he slowly raised his head, and his clear sweet voice rose into the sky like a quivering flame of fire. He began with the ancient legend of the kingly line lost in the haze of the past, and brought it down through its long course of heroism and matchless generosity to the present age. He fixed his gaze on the king's face, and all the vast and unexpressed love of the people for the royal house rose like incense in his song, and enwreathed the throne on all sides. These were his last words when, trembling, he took his seat, "My master, I may be beaten in play of words, but not in my love for thee."

Tears filled the eyes of the hearers, and the stone walls shook with cries of victory.

Mocking this popular outburst of feeling, with an august shake of his head and a contemptuous sneer, Pundarik stood up and flung this question to the assembly, "What is there superior to words?" In a moment the hall lapsed into silence again.

With a marvellous display of learning, he proved that the word was in the beginning, that the word was God. He piled up quotations from scriptures, and built a high altar for the word to be seated above all that there is in heaven and in earth. He repeated that question in his mighty voice, "Is there anything superior to words?"

Proudly he looked around him. None dared to accept his challenge, and he slowly took his seat like a lion that had just made a full meal of its victim. The pandits shouted, "Bravo!," the king remained silent with wonder, and the poet Shekhar felt himself of no account by the side of this stupendous learning. The assembly broke up for that day.

Next day, Shekhar began his song. It was of that day when the pipings of love's flute startled for the first time the hushed air of the Vrinda forest. The shepherd women did not know who the player was or whence the music came. Sometimes, it seemed to come from the heart of the south wind, and sometimes from the straying clouds of the hilltops. It came with a message of tryst from the land of the sunrise, and it floated from the verge of sunset with its sigh of sorrow. The stars seemed to be the stops of the instrument that flooded the dreams of the night with melody. The music seemed to burst all at once from all sides, from fields and groves, from the shady lanes and lonely roads, from the melting blue of the sky, from the shimmering green of the grass. They neither knew its meaning nor could they find words to give utterance to the desire of their hearts. Tears filled their eyes, and their life seemed to long for a death that would be its consummation.

Shekhar forgot his audience, forgot the trial of his strength with a rival. He stood alone amid his thoughts that rustled and quivered round him like leaves in a summer breeze, and sang the song of the flute. He had in his mind the vision of an image that had taken its shape from a shadow, and the echo of a faint tinkling sound of a distant footstep.

He took his seat. His hearers trembled with the sadness of an indefinable delight, immense and vague, and they forgot to applaud him. As this feeling died away Pundarik stood up before the throne and challenged his rival to define who this lover was and who was the beloved. He arrogantly looked around him, smiled at his followers and then put the question again, "Who is Krishna, the lover, and who is Radha, the beloved?"

He then began to analyse the roots of those names, and various interpretations of their meanings. He brought before the bewildered audience all the intricacies of the different schools of metaphysics with consummate skill. Each letter of those names he divided from its fellow, and then pursued them with a relentless logic till they fell to the dust in confusion, to be caught up again and restored to a meaning never before imagined by the subtlest of word-mongers.

The pandits were in ecstasy, they applauded vociferously and the crowd followed them, deluded into the certainty that they had witnessed, that day, the last shred of the curtains of truth torn to pieces before their eyes by a prodigy of intellect. The performance of his tremendous feat so delighted them that they forgot to ask themselves if there was any truth behind it after all.

The king's mind was overwhelmed with wonder. The atmosphere was completely cleared of all illusion of music, and the vision of the world around seemed to be changed from its freshness of tender green to the solidity of a high road levelled and made hard with crushed stones.

To the people assembled their own poet appeared a mere boy in comparison with this giant, who walked with such ease, knocking down difficulties at each step in the world of words and thoughts. It became evident to them for the first time that the poems Shekhar wrote were absurdly simple, and it must be a mere accident that they did not write them themselves. They were neither new, nor difficult, nor instructive, nor necessary.

The king tried to goad his poet with keen glances, silently inciting him to make a final effort. But Shekhar took no notice, and remained fixed to his seat.

The king in anger came down from his throne, took off his pearl chain and put it on Pundarik's head. Everybody in the hall cheered. From the upper balcony came a slight sound of the movements of rustling robes and waist-chains hung with golden bells. Shekhar rose from his seat and left the hall.

It was a dark night of waning moon. The poet Shekhar took down his manuscripts from his shelves and heaped them on the floor. Some of them contained his earliest writings, which he had almost forgotten. He turned over the pages, reading passages here and there. They all seemed to him poor and trivial – mere words and childish rhymes!

One by one he tore his books to fragments, and threw them into a vessel containing fire, and said, "To thee, to thee, O my beauty, my fire! Thou hast been burning in my heart all these futile years. If my life were a piece of gold it would come out of its trial brighter, but it is a trodden turf of grass, and nothing remains of it but this handful of ashes."

The night wore on. Shekhar opened wide his windows. He spread upon his bed the white flowers that he loved, the jasmines, tuberoses and chrysanthemums, and brought into his bedroom all the lamps he had in his house and lighted them. Then mixing with honey the juice of some poisonous root he drank it and lay down on his bed.

Golden anklets tinkled in the passage outside the door, and a subtle perfume came into the room with the breeze.

The poet with his eyes shut said, "My lady, have you taken pity upon your servant at last and come to see him?"

The answer came in a sweet voice, "My poet, I have come."

Shekhar opened his eyes and saw before his bed the figure of a woman.

His sight was dim and blurred. And it seemed to him that the image made of a shadow that he had ever kept throned in the secret shrine of his heart had come into the outer world in his last moment to gaze upon his face.

The woman said, "I am Princess Ajita."

The poet with a great effort sat up on his bed.

The princess whispered into his ear, "The king has not done you justice. It was you who won at the combat, my poet, and I have come to crown you with the crown of victory."

She took the garland of flowers from her own neck, and put it on his hair, and the poet fell down upon his bed stricken by death.

3
The Homecoming

Among the boys of the village, Phatik Chakravorti was ringleader. A new mischief got into his head. There was a heavy log lying on the mud-flat of the river waiting to be shaped into a mast for a boat. He decided that they should all work together to shift the log by main force from its place and roll it away. The owner of the log would be angry and surprised, and they would all enjoy the fun. Every one seconded the proposal, and it was carried unanimously.

But just as the fun was about to begin, Makhan, Phatik's younger brother, sauntered up, and sat down on the log in front of them all without a word. The boys were puzzled for a moment. He was pushed, rather timidly, by one of the boys and told to get up but he remained quite unconcerned. He appeared like a young philosopher meditating on the futility of games. Phatik was furious. "Makhan," he cried, "if you don't get down this minute I'll thrash you!"

Makhan only moved to a more comfortable position.

Now, if Phatik was to keep his regal dignity before the public, it was clear he ought to carry out his threat. But his courage failed him at the crisis. His fertile brain, however, rapidly seized upon a new manoeuvre which would discomfit his brother and afford his followers an added amusement. He gave the word of command to roll the log and Makhan over together. Makhan heard the order, and made it a point of honour to stick on. But he overlooked the fact, like those who attempt earthly fame in other matters, that there was peril in it.

The boys began to heave at the log with all their might, calling out, "One, two, three, go." At the word "go" the log went, and with it went Makhan's philosophy, glory and all.

All the other boys shouted themselves hoarse with delight. But Phatik was a little frightened. He knew what was coming and sure enough, Makhan rose from Mother Earth blind as fate and screaming like the furies. He rushed at Phatik and scratched his face and beat him and kicked him, and then went crying home. The first act of the drama was over.

Phatik wiped his face, and sat down on the edge of a sunken barge on the river bank, and began to chew a piece of grass. A boat came up to the landing, and a middle-aged man, with grey hair and dark moustache, stepped on shore. He saw the boy sitting there doing nothing, and asked him where the Chakravortis lived. Phatik went on chewing the grass, and said, "Over there," but it was quite impossible to tell where he pointed. The stranger asked him again. He swung his legs to and fro on the side of the barge, and said, "Go and find out," and continued to chew the grass as before.

But now a servant came down from the house, and told Phatik that his mother wanted him. Phatik refused to move. But the servant was the master on this occasion. He took Phatik up roughly, and carried him, kicking and struggling in impotent rage.

When Phatik came into the house, his mother saw him. She called out angrily, "So you have been hitting Makhan again?"

Phatik answered indignantly, "No, I haven't, who told you that?"

His mother shouted, "Don't tell lies! You have."

Phatik said suddenly, "I tell you, I haven't. You ask Makhan!" But Makhan thought it best to stick to his previous statement. He said, "Yes, mother. Phatik did hit me."

Phatik's patience was already exhausted. He could not hear this injustice. He rushed at Makhan, and hammered him with blows, "Take that" he cried, "and that, and that, for telling lies."

His mother took Makhan's side in a moment, and pulled Phatik away, beating him with her hands. When Phatik pushed her aside, she shouted out, "You little villain! Would you hit your own mother?"

It was just at this critical juncture that the grey-haired stranger arrived. He asked what the matter was. Phatik looked sheepish and ashamed.

But when his mother stepped back and looked at the stranger, her anger was changed to surprise. For she recognised her brother, and cried, "Why, Dada! Where have you come from?" As she said these words, she bowed to the ground and touched his feet. Her brother had gone away soon after she had married, and he had started business in Bombay. His sister had lost her husband while he was in Bombay. Bishambar had now come back to Calcutta, and had at once made enquiries about his sister. He had then hastened to see her as soon as he found out where she was.

The next few days were full of rejoicing. The brother asked about the education of the two boys. He was told by his sister that Phatik was a perpetual nuisance. He was lazy, disobedient, and wild. But Makhan was as good as gold, as quiet as a lamb, and very fond of reading. Bishambar kindly offered to take Phatik off his sister's hands, and educate him with his own children in Calcutta. The widowed mother readily agreed. When his uncle asked Phatik if he would like to go to Calcutta with him, his joy knew no bounds, and he said, "Oh, yes uncle!" In a way that made it quite clear that he meant it.

It was an immense relief to the mother to get rid of Phatik. She had a prejudice against the boy, and no love was lost between the two brothers. She was in daily fear that he would either drown Makhan some day in the river, or break his head in a fight, or run him into some danger or other. At the same time she was somewhat distressed to see Phatik's extreme eagerness to get away.

Phatik, as soon as all was settled, kept asking his uncle every minute when they were to start. He was on pins and needles all day long with excitement, and lay awake most of the night. He bequeathed to Makhan, in perpetuity, his fishing-rod, his big kite and his marbles. Indeed, at this time of departure his generosity towards Makhan was unbounded.

When they reached Calcutta, Phatik made the acquaintance of his aunt for the first time. She was by no means pleased with this unnecessary addition to her family. She found her own three boys quite enough to manage without taking any one else. It was terribly upsetting to bring a village lad of fourteen into their family. Bishambar should really have thought twice before committing such an indiscretion.

In this world of human affairs, there is no worse nuisance than a boy at the age of fourteen. He is neither ornamental nor useful. It is impossible to shower affection on him as on a little boy, and he is always getting in the way. If he talks with a childish lisp he is called a baby, and if he answers in a grown-up way he is called impertinent. In fact, any talk at all from him is resented. Then he is at the unattractive, growing age. He grows out of his clothes with indecent haste, his voice grows hoarse and breaks and quavers, his face grows suddenly angular and unsightly. It is easy to excuse the shortcomings of early childhood, but it is hard to tolerate even unavoidable lapses in a boy of fourteen. The lad himself becomes painfully self-conscious. When he talks with elderly people he is either unduly forward, or else so unduly shy that he appears ashamed of his very existence.

Yet, it is at this very age when in his heart of hearts a young lad most craves for recognition and love, and he becomes the devoted slave of anyone who shows him consideration. But none dare openly love him, for that would be regarded as an undue indulgence and therefore, bad for the boy. So, what with scolding and chiding, he becomes very much like a stray dog that has lost his master.

For a boy of fourteen, his own home is the only paradise. To live in a strange house with strange people is little short of torture, while the height of bliss is to receive the kind looks of women, and never to be slighted by them.

It was anguish to Phatik to be the unwelcome guest in his aunt's house, despised by this elderly woman, and slighted, on every occasion. If she ever asked him to do anything for her, he would be so overjoyed that he would overdo it, and then she would tell him not to be so stupid, but to get on with his lessons.

The cramped atmosphere of neglect in his aunt's house oppressed Phatik so much that he felt that he could hardly breathe. He wanted to go out into the open country and fill his lungs and breathe freely. But there was no open country to go to. Surrounded on all sides by Calcutta houses and walls, he would dream night after night of his village home, and long to be back there. He remembered the glorious meadow where he used to fly his kite all day long, the broad river-banks where he would wonder about the livelong day singing and shouting for joy, the narrow brook where he could go and dive and swim at any time he liked. He thought of his band of boy companions over whom he was despot, and above all, the memory of that tyrant mother of his, who had such a prejudice against him, occupied his day and night. A kind of physical love like that of animals, a longing to be in the presence of the one who is loved, an inexpressible wistfulness during absence, a silent cry of the inmost heart for the mother, like the lowing of a calf in the twilight, this love which was almost an animal instinct, agitated the shy, nervous, lean, uncouth and ugly boy. No one could understand it, but it preyed upon his mind continually.

There was no more backward boy in the whole school than Phatik. He gaped and remained silent when the teacher asked him a question, and like an overladen ass patiently suffered all the blows that came down on his back. When other boys were out at play, he stood wistfully by the window and gazed at the roofs of the distant houses. And if by chance he espied children playing on the open terrace of any roof, his heart would ache with longing.

One day, he summoned up all his courage and asked, "Uncle, when can I go home?"

His uncle answered, "Wait till the holidays come." But the holidays would not come till November, and there was a long time still to wait.

One day Phatik lost his lesson-book. Even with the help of books he had found it very difficult indeed to prepare his lesson. Now it was impossible. Day after day the teacher would cane him unmercifully. His condition became so abjectly miserable that even his cousins were ashamed to own him. They began to jeer and insult him more than the other boys. He went to his aunt at last and told her that he had lost his book.

His aunt pursed her lips in contempt and said, "You great clumsy, country lout. How can I afford, with all my family, to buy you new books five times a month?"

That night on his way back from school, Phatik had a bad headache with a fit of shivering. He felt he was going to have an attack of malarial fever. His one great fear was that he would be a nuisance to his aunt.

Next morning, Phatik was nowhere to be seen. All searches in the neighbourhood proved futile. The rain had been pouring in torrents all night, and those who went out in search of the boy got drenched through to the skin. At last, Bisbamber asked for help from the police.

At the end of the day, a police van stopped at the door before the house. It was still raining and the streets were all flooded. Two constables brought out Phatik in their arms and placed him before Bishambar. He was wet through from head to foot, muddy all over, his face and eyes flushed red with fever, and his limbs all trembling. Bishambar carried him in his arms and took him into the inner apartments. When his wife saw him, she exclaimed, "What a heap of trouble this boy has given us. Hadn't you better send him home?"

Phatik heard her words, and sobbed out loud, "Uncle, I was just going home, but they dragged me back again."

The fever rose very high, and all that night the boy was delirious. Bishambar brought in a doctor. Phatik opened his eyes flushed with fever, and looked up to the ceiling, and said vacantly, "Uncle, have the holidays come yet? May I go home?"

Bishambar wiped the tears from his own eyes, and took Phatik's lean and burning hands in his own, and sat by him through the night. The boy began to mutter again. At last, his voice became excited, "Mother!," he cried, "Don't beat me like that! Mother! I am telling the truth!"

Next day, Phatik became conscious for a short time. He turned his eyes about the room as if expecting someone to come. At last, with an air of disappointment, his head sank back on the pillow. He turned his face to the wall with a deep sigh.

Bishambar knew his thoughts, so bending down his head, he whispered, "Phatik, I have sent for your mother." The day went by. The doctor said in a troubled voice that the boy's condition was very critical.

Phatik began to cry out, "By the mark! – three fathoms. By the mark – four fathoms. By the mark..." He had heard the sailor on the river-steamer calling out the mark on the plumb-line. Now he was himself plumbing an unfathomable sea.

Later that day, Phatik's mother burst into the room like a whirlwind, and began to toss from side to side and moan and cry in a loud voice.

Bishambar tried to calm her agitation, but she flung herself on the bed, and cried, "Phatik, my darling, my darling."

Phatik stopped his restless movements for a moment. His hands ceased beating up and down. He said, "Eh?"

The mother cried again, "Phatik, my darling, my darling."

Phatik slowly turned his head and said, "Mother, the holidays have come."

4
Vision

I

When I was a very young wife, I gave birth to a dead child and came near to death myself. I recovered strength very slowly, and my eyesight became weaker and weaker.

My husband at this time was studying medicine. He was not altogether sorry to have a chance of testing his medical knowledge on me. So he began to treat my eyes himself.

My elder brother was studying for his law examination. One day he came to see me and was alarmed at my condition.

"What are you doing?" he said to my husband. "You would ruin Kumo's eyes. You ought to consult a good doctor at once."

My husband said irritably, "Why! What can a good doctor do more than I am doing? The case is quite a simple one, and the remedies are all well known."

Dada answered with scorn, "I suppose you think there is no difference between you and the Professor in your own medical college."

My husband replied angrily, "If you ever get married, and there is a dispute about your wife's property, you won't take my advice about law. Why do you come now to advise me about medicine?"

While they were quarrelling, I was saying to myself that it was always the poor grass that suffered most when two kings went to war. There was a dispute going on between these two, and I had to bear the brunt of it.

It also seemed to me very unfair that, when my family had given me in marriage, they should interfere afterwards. After all, my pleasure and pain are my husband's concern, not theirs.

From that day onwards, merely over this trifling matter of my eyes, the bond between my husband and Dada was strained.

To my surprise one afternoon, while my husband was away, Dada brought a doctor in to see me. He examined my eyes very carefully and looked grave. He said that further neglect would be dangerous. He wrote out a prescription and Dada went out for the medicines at once. When the strange doctor had gone, I implored my Dada not to interfere. I was sure that only evil would come from the stealthy visits of a doctor.

I was surprised at myself for plucking up courage to speak to my brother like that. I had always hitherto been afraid of him. I am also sure that Dada was surprised at my boldness. He was silent for a while, and then said to me, "Very well, Kumo. I won't call in the doctor anymore. But when the medicine comes you must take it."

Dada went away. The medicine came from the chemist. I took the bottles, powders, prescriptions and all – and threw it down the well!

My husband had been irritated by Dada's interference, and he began to treat my eyes with greater diligence than ever. He tried all sorts of remedies. I bandaged my eyes as he told me, I wore his coloured glasses, I put in his drops, I took all his powders, I even drank the cod-liver oil he gave me, though my gorge rose against it.

Each time he came back from the hospital, he would ask me anxiously how I felt, and I would answer, "Oh! Much better." Indeed, I became an expert in self-delusion. When I found that the water in my eyes was still increasing, I would console myself with the thought that it was a good thing to get rid of bad fluids and when it decreased, I was elated at my husband's skill.

But after a while, the agony became unbearable. My eyesight faded away, and I had continual headaches day and night. I saw how much alarmed my husband was getting. I gathered from his manner that he was casting about for a pretext to call in a doctor. So I hinted that it might be as well to call one in.

The moment I hinted to call a doctor, I felt that he was greatly relieved. He called in an English doctor that very day. I do not know what they discussed, but I gathered that the Sahib had spoken very sharply to my husband.

He remained silent for some time after the doctor had gone. I took his hands in mine and said, "What an ill-mannered brute that was! Why didn't you call an Indian doctor? That would have been much better. Do you think that man knows better than you do about my eyes?"

My husband was silent for a moment, and then said with a broken voice, "Kumo, your eyes must be operated on."

I pretended to be vexed with him for concealing the fact from me so long.

"Here you have known this all the time," said I, "and yet you have said nothing about it! Do you think I am such a baby to be afraid of an operation?"

By hearing this, he regained back his spirits and said, "There are very few men who are heroic enough to look forward to an operation without shrinking."

I laughed at him, "Yes, that is so. Men are heroic only before their wives!"

He looked at me gravely and said, "You are perfectly right. We men are dreadfully vain."

I laughed away his seriousness, "Are you sure you can beat us women even in vanity?"

When Dada came, I took him aside, "Dada, that treatment your doctor recommended would have done me a world of good, but unfortunately. I mistook the mixture for the lotion. And since that day, my eyes have grown steadily worse, and now an operation is needed."

Dada said to me, "You were under your husband's treatment, and that is why I gave up coming to visit you."

"No!" I answered. "In reality, I was secretly treating myself in accordance with your doctor's directions."

Oh! How many lies we women have to tell! When we are mothers, we tell lies to pacify our children, and when we are wives, we tell lies to pacify the fathers of our children. We are never free from this necessity.

My deception had the effect of bringing about a better feeling between my husband and Dada. Dada blamed himself for asking me to keep a secret from my husband, and my husband regretted that he had not taken my brother's advice at the first.

At last, with the consent of both, an English doctor came and operated on my left eye. That eye, however, was too weak to bear the strain, and the last flickering glimmer of light went out. Then the other eye gradually lost itself in darkness.

One day my husband came to my bedside, "I cannot brazen it out before you any longer," said he, "Kumo, it is I who have ruined your eyes."

I felt that his voice was choking with tears, and so I took up his right hand in both of mine and said, "Why! you did exactly what was right. You have dealt only with that which was your very own. Just imagine, if some strange doctor had come and taken away my eyesight. What consolation should I have had then? But now I can feel that all has happened for the best, and my great comfort is to know that it is at your hands I have lost my eyes. When Ramchandra found one lotus too few with which to worship God, he offered both his eyes in place of the lotus. And I have dedicated my eyes to my God. From now on, whenever you see something that symbolizes joy, you must describe it to me, and I will feed upon your words as a sacred gift left over from your vision."

I do not mean, of course, that I said all this there and then, for it is impossible to speak these things at a spur of the moment. But I used to think over words like these for days and days together. And when I was very depressed, or if at any time the light of my devotion became dim, and I pitied my evil fate, then I made my mind utter these sentences, one by one, as a child repeats a story that is told. And so I could breathe once more the serener air of peace and love.

At the very time of our talk together, I said enough to show my husband what was in my heart.

"Kumo," he said to me, "the mischief I have done by my folly can never be made good. But I can do one thing. I can ever remain by your side, and try to make up for your want of vision as much as is in my power."

"No!" said I, "that will never do. I shall not ask you to turn your house into a hospital for the blind. There is only one thing to be done, you must marry again."

As I tried to explain to him that this was necessary, my voice broke a little. I coughed and tried to hide my emotion, but he burst out saying, "Kumo, I know I am a fool, and a braggart, and all that, but I am not a villain! If ever I marry again, I swear to you – I swear to you the most solemn oath by my family god, Gopinath – may that most hated of all sins, the sin of parricide, fall on my head!"

Ah! I should have never ever allowed him to swear that dreadful oath. But tears were choking my voice, and I could not say a word for insufferable joy. I hid my blind face in my pillows, and sobbed, and sobbed again.

"Ah!" said I, "Why did you take such a terrible oath? Do you think I asked you to marry again for your own sordid pleasure? No! I was thinking of myself, for she could perform those services which were mine to give you when I had my sight."

"Services!" said he, "Services! Those can be done by servants. Do you think I am mad enough to bring a slave into my house and bid her share the throne with my Goddess?"

I said to myself, "I am no longer able to serve him in the lower world of household cares. But I shall rise to a higher region. I shall bring down blessings from above. No more lies! No more deceptions for me! All the littlenesses and hypocrisies of my former life shall be banished forever!"

That day, the whole day through, I felt a conflict going on within me. The joy of the thought, that after this solemn oath it was impossible for my husband to marry again, fixed its roots deep in my heart, and I could not tear them out. But the new Goddess, who had taken her new throne in me said, "The time might come when it would be good for your husband to break his oath and marry again." But the woman, who was within me said, "But all the same, an oath is an oath and there is no way out." The Goddess within me answered, "That is no reason why you should exult over it." But the woman, who was within me replied, "What you say is quite true, no doubt, all the same he has taken his oath." And the same story went on again and again. At last, the Goddess frowned in silence and the darkness of a horrible fear came down upon me.

My repentant husband would not let the servants do my work, he must do it all himself. At first, it gave me unbounded delight to be dependent on him for every little thing. It was a means of keeping him by my side, and my desire to have him with me had become intense since my blindness. That share of his presence, which my eyes had lost, my other senses craved. When he was absent from my side, I would feel as if

I were hanging in mid-air, and had lost my hold of all things tangible.

Formerly, when my husband came back late from the hospital, I used to open my window and gaze at the road. That road was the link which connected his world with mine. Now, when I had lost that link through my blindness, all my body would go out to seek him. The bridge that united us had given way, and there was now this unsurpassable chasm. When he left my side the gulf seemed to yawn wide open. I could only wait for the time when he should cross back again from his own shore to mine.

But such intense longing and such utter dependence can never be good. A wife is a burden enough to a man, in all conscience, and to add to it the burden of this blindness was to make his life unbearable. I vowed that I would suffer alone, and never wrap my husband round in the folds of my all-pervading darkness.

Within an incredibly short space of time, I managed to train myself to do all my household duties with the help of touch and sound and smell. In fact, I soon found that I could get on with greater skill than before, for sight often distracts rather than helps us. So it came to pass that when these roving eyes of mine could do their work no longer, all the other senses took up their several duties with quietude and completeness.

When I had gained experience with constant practice, I would not let my husband do any more household duties for me. He complained bitterly at first that I was depriving him of his penance. But, this did not convince me. Whatever he might say, I could feel that he had a real sense of relief when these household duties were over. To serve a blind wife daily can never make up the life of a man.

II

My husband finished his medical course and went away from Calcutta to practise as a doctor. In the country, I felt the joy as if I was restored to the arms of my mother. I had left my village birthplace for Calcutta when I was eight years old. Since then ten years had passed and in the great city, the memory of my village home had grown dimmer. As long as I had eyesight, Calcutta with its busy life screened from view the memory of my early days. But when I lost my eyesight I knew for the first time that Calcutta allured only the eyes, but could not fill the mind. And now, in my blindness, the scenes of my childhood shone out once more, like stars that appear one by one in the evening sky at the end of the day.

It was the beginning of November when we left Calcutta for Harsingpur. The place was new to me, but the scents and sounds of the countryside pressed round and embraced me. The morning breeze coming fresh from the newly ploughed land, the sweet and tender smell of the flowering mustard, the shepherd-boy's flute sounding in the distance, even the creaking noise of the bullock-cart, as it groaned over the broken village road, filled my world with delight. The memory of my past life, with all its ineffable fragrance and sound, became a living present to me, and my blind eyes could not tell me I was wrong. I went back and lived over again my childhood. Only one thing was absent, my mother was not with me.

I could see my home with the large peepal trees growing along the edge of the village pool. I could picture in my mind's eye my old grandmother seated on the ground with her thin wisps of hair untied, warming her back in the sun as she made the little round lentil balls to be dried and used for cooking. But somehow I could not recall the songs she used to croon to herself in her weak and quavering voice. In the evening, whenever I heard the lowing of cattle, I could almost watch the figure of my mother going around the sheds with a lighted lamp in her hand. The smell of the wet fodder and the pungent smoke of the straw fire would enter into my very heart. And in the distance, I seemed to hear the clanging of the temple bell wafted up by the breeze from the river bank.

Calcutta, with all its turmoil and gossip, curdles the heart. There, all the beautiful duties of life lose their freshness and innocence. I remember one day, when a friend of mine came in and said to me, "Kumo, why don't you feel angry? If I had been treated like you by my husband, I would never look upon his face again."

She tried to make me indignant because he had been so long calling in a doctor.

"My blindness," said I, "was itself a sufficient evil. Why should I make it worse by allowing hatred to grow up against my husband?"

My friend shook her head in great contempt when she heard such old-fashioned talk from the lips of a mere chit of a girl. She went away in disdain. But whatever might be my answer at the time, such words as these left their poison, and the venom was never wholly got out of the soul, when once they had been uttered.

So you see, Calcutta with its never-ending gossip, does harden the heart. But when I came back to the country all my earlier hopes and faiths, all that I held true in life during childhood, became fresh and bright once more. God came to me and filled my heart and my world. I bowed to Him and said, "It is well that thou hast taken away my eyes. Thou art with me."

Ah! But I said more than was right. It was a presumption to say, "Thou art with me." All we can say is this, "I must be true to thee." Even when nothing is left for us, still we have to go on living.

III

We passed a few happy months together. My husband gained some reputation in his profession as a doctor. And the money came with it.

But with money comes numerous unexpected mishappenings. I cannot point to any one event, but, because the blind have keener perceptions than other people, I could discern the change which came over my husband along with the increase of wealth.

He had a keen sense of justice when he was younger and had often told me of his great desire to help the poor when once he obtained a practice of his own. He had a noble contempt for those in his profession who would not feel the pulse of a poor patient before collecting his fee. But now I noticed a difference. He had become strangely hard. Once, when a poor woman came and begged him, out of charity, to save the life of her only child, he bluntly refused. And when I insisted him to help her, he did his work perfunctorily.

When we were less wealthy, my husband used to dislike sharp practices in money matters. He was scrupulously honourable in such things. But since he had got a large account at the bank he was often closeted for hours with some scamp of a landlord's agent, for purposes which clearly boded no good.

Where has he drifted? What has become of this husband of mine – the husband, I knew before I was blind, and enshrined me on the throne of a Goddess? Those whom a sudden gust of passion brings down to the dust can rise up again with a new strong impulse of goodness. But those who day by day, become dried up in the very fibre of their moral being, choked by some outer parasitic growth lets out a feeling of deadness which knows no healing.

The separation caused by blindness is the merest physical trifle. But, ah! it suffocates me to find that he is no longer with me, where he stood with me in that hour when we both knew that I was blind. That is a separation indeed!

I, with my love fresh and my faith unbroken, have kept to the shelter of my heart's inner shrine. But my husband has left the cool shade of those things that are ageless and unfading. He is fast disappearing into the barren, waterless waste in his mad thirst for gold.

Sometimes I doubt that things are not as bad as they seem and perhaps I exaggerate because I am blind. It may be that, if my eyesight were unimpaired, I would have accepted the world as I found it. This, at any rate, was the light in which my husband looked at all my moods and fancies.

One day, an old Musalman came to the house. He asked my husband to visit his little grand-daughter. I could hear the old man say, "Baba, I am a poor man, but come with me, and Allah will do you good." My husband answered coldly, "What Allah will do won't help, I want to know what you can do for me."

When I heard it, I wondered in my mind why God had not made me deaf as well as blind. The old man heaved a deep sigh and departed. I sent my maid to fetch him to my room. I met him at the door of the inner apartment, and put some money into his hand.

"Please take this from me," said I, "for your little grand-daughter, and get a trustworthy doctor to look after her. And pray for my husband."

That day, I could not take food at all. In the afternoon, when my husband woke up from sleep, he asked me, "Why do you look so pale?"

I was about to say, as I used to do in the past, "Oh! It's nothing," but those days of deception were over, and I decided to speak to him plainly.

"I have been hesitating," I said, "for days together to tell you something. It has been hard to think out what exactly it was I wanted to say. Even now I may not be able to explain what I had in my mind. But I am sure you know what has happened. Our lives have drifted apart."

My husband laughed forcibly and said, "Change is the law of nature."

I said to him, "I know that. But there are some things that are eternal."

Then he became serious.

"There are many women," said he, "who have a real cause for sorrow. There are some, whose husbands do not earn money. There are others whose husbands do not love them. But you are making yourself wretched about nothing at all."

It became clear to me that my blindness had conferred on me the power of seeing a world which is beyond all change. Yes! It is true. I am not like other women. And my husband will never understand me.

IV

Our two lives went on with their dull routine for some time. Then there was a break in the monotony. An aunt of my husband came to pay us a visit.

The first thing she blurted out after our first greeting was this, "Well, Kumo, it's a great pity you have become blind, but why do you impose your own affliction on your husband? You must get him to another wife."

There was an awkward pause. If my husband had only said something in jest or laughed in her face, all would have been over. But he stammered and hesitated, and said at last nervously, "Do you really think so? Really, Aunt, you shouldn't talk like that."

His aunt appealed to me, "Was I wrong, Kumo?"

I laughed a hollow laugh.

I said, "Shouldn't you consult someone more competent to decide? The pickpocket never asks permission from the man whose pocket he is going to pick."

"You are quite right," she replied blandly, "Abinash, my dear, let us have our little conference in private. What do you say to that?"

After a few days, my husband asked her, in my presence, if she knew of any girl of a decent family who could come and help me in my household work. He knew quite well that I needed no help. I kept silence.

"Oh! There are heaps of them. My cousin has a daughter who is just of the marriageable age, and as nice a girl as you could wish. Her people would be only too glad to secure you as a husband," replied his aunt.

Again there came from him that forced, hesitating laugh, and he said, "But I never mentioned marriage."

"How could you expect," asked his aunt, "a girl of a decent family to come and live in your house without marriage?"

He had to admit that this was reasonable and remained nervously silent.

I stood alone within the closed doors of my blindness after he had gone, and called upon my God and prayed, "O God, save my husband."

When I was coming out of the household shrine from my morning worship a few days later, his aunt took hold of both my hands warmly and said, "Kumo, here is the girl, about whom we were talking about the other day. Her name is Hemangini. She will be delighted to meet you. Hemo, come here and introduce yourself to your sister."

My husband entered the room at the same moment. He feigned surprise when he saw the strange girl and was about to retire. But his aunt said, "Abinash, my dear, what are you running away for? There is no need to do that. Here is my cousin's daughter, Hemangini has come to see you. Hemo, greet him!"

As if taken by surprise, he began to ply his aunt with questions about 'when, why and how' of the new arrival.

I saw the hollowness of the whole thing, and took Hemangini by the hand and led her to my own room. I gently stroked her face and arms and hair and found that she was about fifteen years old and very beautiful.

As I felt her face, she suddenly burst out laughing and said, "Why! What are you doing? Are you hypnotising me?"

That sweet ringing laughter of hers swept away in a moment all the dark clouds that stood between us. I threw my right arm about her neck.

"Dear one," said I, "I am trying to see you." And again I stroked her soft face with my left hand.

"Trying to see me?" she said, with a new burst of laughter. "Am I like a vegetable marrow, grown in your garden, that you want to feel me all round to see how soft I am?"

I suddenly bethought me that she did not know I had lost my sight.

"Sister, I am blind," said I.

She was silent. I could feel her big young eyes, full of curiosity, peering into my face. I knew they were full of pity. Then she grew thoughtful and puzzled, and said, after a short pause, "Oh! I see now. That was the reason your husband invited his aunt to come and stay here."

"No!" I replied, "You are quite mistaken. He did not ask her to come. She came of her own accord."

43

Hemangini went off into a peal of laughter. "That's just like my aunt," said she, "Oh, wasn't it nice of her to come without an invitation? But now that she's here, you won't get her to move for some time, I can assure you!"

Then she paused and looked puzzled.

"But why did father send me?" she asked. "Can you tell me that?"

The aunt had come into the room while we were talking. Hemangini said to her, "When are you thinking of going back, Aunt?"

The aunt looked very much upset.

"What a question to ask!" said she, "I've never seen such a restless body as you. We've only just come, and you ask when we're going back!"

"It is all very well for you," Hemangini said, "for this house belongs to your relatives. But what about me? Let me tell you that I can't stop here." Then she held my hand and said, "What do you think, dear?"

I drew her close to my heart but said nothing. The aunt was in great difficulty. She felt the situation was getting beyond her control, so she proposed that she and her niece should go out together to bathe.

"No! both of us will go together," said Hemangini, clinging to me. The aunt gave in, fearing opposition if she tried to drag her away.

Going down to the river Hemangini asked me, "Why don't you have children?"

I was startled by her question, and answered, "How can I tell? My God has not given me any. That is the reason."

"No! That's not the reason," said Hemangini quickly. "You must have committed some sin. Look at my aunt. She is childless. It must be because her heart has some wickedness. But what wickedness is in your heart?"

The words hurt me. I have no solution to offer for the problem of evil. I sighed deeply, and said in the silence of my soul, "My God! Thou knowest the reason."

"Gracious goodness!," cried Hemangini, "What are you sighing for? No one ever takes me seriously."

And her laughter pealed across the river.

V

After this, I found out that there were constant interruptions in my husband's professional duties. He refused all calls from a distance and would hurry away from his patients, even when they were close at hand.

Formerly it was only during the mid-day meals and at nighttime that he could come into the inner apartment. But now, with unnecessary anxiety for his aunt's comfort, he began to visit her at all hours of the day. I knew at once that he had come to her room when I heard her shouting for Hemangini to bring in a glass of water. At first, the girl would do what she was told but later on, she refused altogether.

Then the aunt would call, in an endearing voice, "Hemo! Hemo! Hemangini!" But the girl would cling to me with an impulse of pity. A sense of dread and sadness would keep her silent. Sometimes she would shrink towards me like a hunted thing, who scarcely knew what was coming.

About this time, my brother came down from Calcutta to visit me. I knew how keen his powers of observation were, and what a hard judge he was. I feared my husband would be put on his defence, and have to stand his trial before him. So I endeavoured to hide the true situation behind a mask of noisy cheerfulness. But I am afraid I overdid the part, it was unnatural for me.

My husband began to fidget openly and asked how long my brother was going to stay. At last, his impatience became little short of insulting, and my brother could not help but had to leave. Before going, he placed his hand on my head and kept it there for some time. I noticed that his hand shook, and a tear fell from his eyes, as he silently gave me his blessing.

I well remember that it was an evening in April and a market-day. People who had come into the town were going back home from the market.

There was the feeling of an impending storm in the air, the smell of the wet earth and the moisture in the wind were all-pervading. I never keep a lighted lamp in my bedroom, when I am alone, lest my clothes should catch fire, or some accident might happen. I sat on the floor in my darkroom and called upon the God of my blind world.

"O my Lord," I cried, "thy face is hidden. I cannot see. I am blind. I hold tight this broken rudder of a heart till my hands bleed. The waves have become too strong for me. How long wilt thou try me, my God, how long?"

I kept my head prone upon the bedstead and began to sob. As I did so, I felt the bedstead move a little. The next moment, Hemangini was by my side. She clung to my neck and wiped my tears away silently. I do not know why she had been waiting that evening in the inner room, or why she had been lying alone there in the dusk. She asked me no question. She said no word. She simply placed her cool hand on my forehead, and kissed me, and departed.

Next morning, Hemangini said to her aunt in my presence, "If you want to stay on, you can. But I don't. I'm going away home with our family servant."

The aunt said there was no need for her to go alone, for she was going away also. Then smilingly and mincingly she brought out, from a plush case, a ring set with pearls.

"Look, Hemo," said she, "what a beautiful ring my Abinash brought for you."

Hemangini snatched the ring from her hand.

"Look, Aunt," she answered quickly, "just see how splendidly I aim." And she flung the ring into the tank outside the window.

The aunt, overwhelmed with alarm, vexation, and surprise, bristled like a hedgehog. She turned to me and held me by the hand.

"Kumo," she repeated again and again, "don't say a word about this childish freak to Abinash. He would be fearfully vexed."

I assured her that she need not fear. Not a word would reach him about it from my lips.

The next day before starting for home Hemangini embraced me and said, "Dearest, keep me in mind, do not forget me."

I stroked her face over and over with my fingers, and said, "Sister, the blind have long memories."

I drew her head towards me, and kissed her hair and her forehead. My world suddenly became grey. All the beauty and laughter and tender youth, which had nestled so close to me, vanished when Hemangini departed. I went groping about with arms outstretched seeking to find out what was left in my deserted world.

My husband came in later. He affected a great relief now that they were gone, but it was exaggerated and empty. He pretended that his aunt's visit had kept him away from work.

Hitherto there had been only the one barrier of blindness between me and my husband. Now another barrier was added-this deliberate silence about Hemangini. He feigned utter indifference, but I knew he was having letters about her.

It was early in May. My maid entered my room one morning, and asked me, "What is all this preparation going on at the landing on the river? Where is master going?"

I knew there was something impending, but I said to the maid, "I can't say."

The maid did not dare to ask me any more questions. She sighed and went away.

Late that night my husband came to me.

"I have to visit a patient in the country," said he, "I shall have to start very early tomorrow morning, and I may have to be away for two or three days."

I got up from my bed. I stood before him, and cried aloud, "Why are you telling me lies?"

My husband stammered out, "What–what lies have I told you?"

I said, "You are going to get married."

He remained silent. For some moments there was no sound in the room. Then I broke the silence,

"Answer me," I cried, "Say yes!"

He answered feebly, "Yes."

I shouted loudly, "No! I shall never allow you. I shall save you from this great disaster, this dreadful sin. If I fail in this, then why am I your wife, and why did I ever worship my God?"

The room remained still as a stone. I dropped on the floor and clung to my husband's knees.

"What have I done?" I asked, "Where have I been lacking? Tell me truly. Why do you want another wife?"

My husband said slowly, "I will tell you the truth. I am afraid of you. Your blindness has enclosed you in its fortress, and I have now no entrance. To me, you are no longer a woman. You are awful as my God. It is becoming difficult to spend each single day with you."

Oh dear, open my heart and see! What am I else but that, – just an ordinary woman? I am the same girl that I was when I was newly-wed, a girl with all her need to believe, to confide, to worship.

I do not recollect exactly the words that I uttered. I only remember that I said, "If I am a true wife, then, may God be my witness, you shall never do this wicked deed, you shall never break your oath. Before you commit such sacrilege, either I shall become a widow, or Hemangini shall die."

Then I fell down on the floor in a swoon. When I came to myself, it was still dark. The birds were silent. My husband had gone.

All that day, I sat at my worship in the sanctuary at the household shrine. In the evening a fierce storm, with thunder and lightning and rain, swept down upon the house and shook it. As I crouched before the shrine, I did not ask my God to save my husband from the storm, though he must have been at that time in peril on the river. I prayed that whatever might happen to me, my husband might be saved from this great sin.

Night passed. The whole of the next day I kept my seat at worship. When it was evening there was the noise of shaking and beating at the door. When the door was broken open, they found me lying unconscious on the ground and carried me to my room.

When I came to myself, at last, I heard someone whispering in my ear, "Sister?"

I found that I was lying in my room with my head on Hemangini's lap. When my head moved, I heard her dress rustle. It was the sound of bridal silk.

O my God, my God! My prayer has gone unheeded! My husband has fallen!

Hemangini bent her head low, and said in a sweet whisper, "Sister, dearest, I have come to ask your blessing on our marriage."

At first, my whole body stiffened like the trunk of a tree that has been struck by lightning. Then I sat up, and said, painfully, forcing myself to speak the words, "Why should I not bless you? You have done no wrong."

Hemangini laughed her merry laugh.

"Wrong!" said she, "When you married it was right, and when I marry, you call it wrong!"

I tried to smile in answer to her laughter. I said in my mind, "My prayer is not the final thing in this world. His will is all. Let the blows descend upon my head, but may they leave my faith and hope in God untouched."

Hemangini bowed to me and touched my feet. "May you be happy," said I and blessed her saying, "and enjoy unbroken prosperity."

Hemangini was still unsatisfied.

"Dearest sister," she said, "a blessing for me is not enough. You must make our happiness complete. You must, with those saintly hands of yours, accept into your home my husband also. Let me bring him to you."

I said, "Yes, bring him to me."

A few moments later I heard a familiar footstep, and the question, "Kumo, how are you?"

I started up, and bowed to the ground, and cried, "Dada!"

Hemangini burst out laughing.

"You still call him elder brother?" she asked, "What nonsense! Call him a younger brother now, and pull his ears and cease him, for he has married me, your younger sister."

Then I understood. My husband had been saved from that great sin. He had not fallen.

I knew my Dada had determined never to marry. And, since my mother had died, there was no sacred wish of hers to implore him to wedlock. But I, his sister, by my sore need had brought it to pass. He had married for my sake.

Tears of joy gushed from my eyes and poured down my cheeks. I tried, but I could not stop them. Dada slowly passed his fingers through my hair. Hemangini clung to me and went on laughing.

I was lying awake in my bed for the best part of the night, waiting with straining anxiety for my husband's return. I could not imagine how he would bear the shock of shame and disappointment.

When it was long past the hour of midnight, slowly my door opened. I sat up on my bed and listened. They were the footsteps of my husband. My heart began to beat wildly. He came up to my bed, held my hand in his.

"Your Dada," said he, "has saved me from destruction. I was being dragged down and down by a moments madness. An infatuation had seized me, from which I seemed unable to escape. God alone knows what a load I was carrying on that day when I entered the boat. The storm came down on the river and covered the sky. In the midst of all fears I had a secret wish in my heart to be drowned, and so disentangle my life from the knot which I had tied it. I reached Mathurganj. There I heard the news which set me free. Your brother had married Hemangini. I cannot tell you with what joy and shame I heard it. I hastened on board the boat again. In that moment of self-revelation, I knew that I could have no happiness except with you. You are a Goddess."

I laughed and cried at the same time and said, "No, no, no! I am not going to be a Goddess any longer I am simply your own little wife. I am an ordinary woman."

"Dearest," he replied, "I have also something I want to say to you. Never again put me to shame by calling me your God."

Next day, the little town became joyous with the sound of conch shells. But nobody made any reference to that night of madness when all was so nearly lost.

5
The Postmaster

The postmaster first took up his duties in the village of Ulapur. Though the village was a small one, there was an indigo factory nearby, and the proprietor, an Englishman, had managed to get a post office established.

Our postmaster belonged to Calcutta. He felt like a fish out of water in this remote village. His office and living-room were in a dark thatched shed, not far from a green, slimy pond, surrounded on all sides by dense growth.

The men employed in the Indigo factory had no leisure, moreover, they were hardly desirable companions for decent folk. Nor is a Calcutta boy an adept in the art of associating with others. Among strangers, he appears either proud or ill at ease. At any rate, the postmaster neither had company, nor had much to do.

At times he tried his hand at writing a verse or two. That the movement of the leaves and the clouds of the sky were enough to fill life with joy—such were the sentiments to which he sought to give expression. But God knows that the poor fellow would have felt it as the gift of a new life, if some genie of the Arabian Nights had in one night swept away the trees, leaves and all, and replaced them with a macadamised road, hiding the clouds from view with rows of tall houses.

The postmaster's salary was small. He had to cook his own meals, which he used to share with Ratan, an orphan girl of the village, who did odd jobs for him.

When in the evening the smoke began to curl up from the village cowsheds, and the cicadas chirped in every bush, when the mendicants of the Baül sect sang their shrill songs in their daily meeting-place, when any poet, who had attempted to watch the movement of the leaves in the dense bamboo thickets, would have felt a ghostly shiver run down his back, the postmaster would light his little lamp, and call out, "Ratan!"

Ratan would sit outside waiting for this call, and, instead of coming in at once, would reply, "Did you call me, sir?"

"What are you doing?" the postmaster would ask.

"I must be going to light the kitchen fire," would be the answer.

And the postmaster would say, "Oh, let the kitchen fire be for a while, light me my pipe first."

At last, Ratan would enter, with puffed-out cheeks, vigorously blowing into a flame a lump of live coal to light the tobacco. Usually, this gives the postmaster an opportunity to converse. "Well, Ratan," perhaps he would begin, "do you remember anything of your mother?" That was a fertile subject. Ratan partly remembered, and partly didn't. Her father had been fonder of her than her mother, and she recollected him more vividly. He used to come home in the evening after his work, and one or two evenings stood out more clearly than others, like pictures in her memory. Ratan would sit on the floor near the postmaster's feet, as memories crowded upon her. She called to mind a little brother that she had—and how on some bygone cloudy day she had played at fishing with him on the edge of the pond, with a twig for a make-believe fishing-rod. Such little incidents would drive out greater events from her mind. Thus, as they talked, it would often get very late, and the postmaster would feel too lazy to do any cooking at all. Ratan would then hastily light the fire and toast some unleavened bread, which, with the cold remnants of the morning meal, was enough for their supper.

During evenings, seated at his desk in the corner of the big empty shed, the postmaster too would call up memories of his own home, of his mother and his sister, of those for whom in his exile his heart was sad,—memories which were always haunting him, but which he could not talk about with the men of the factory, though he found himself naturally recalling them aloud in the presence of the simple little girl. And so it came about that the girl would allude to his people as a mother, brother, and sister as if she had known them all her life. In fact, she had a complete picture of each one of them painted in her little heart.

One noon, during a break in the rains, there was a cool soft breeze blowing, the smell of the damp grass and leaves in the hot sun felt like the warm breathing of the tired earth on one's body. A persistent bird went on all the afternoon repeating the burden of its one complaint in nature's audience chamber.

The postmaster had nothing to do. The shimmer of the freshly washed leaves and the banked-up remnants of the retreating rain-clouds were sights to see, and the postmaster was watching them and thinking to himself, "Oh, if only some kindred soul were near—just one loving human being whom I could hold near my heart!" This was exactly, he went on to think, what that bird was trying to say, and it was the same feeling which the murmuring leaves were striving to express. But no one knows or would believe that such an idea might also take possession of an ill-paid village postmaster in the deep, silent mid-day interval of his work.

The postmaster sighed and called out, "Ratan!" Ratan was then sprawling beneath the guava-tree, busily engaged in eating unripe guavas. At the voice of her master, she ran up breathlessly, saying, "Were you calling me, Dada?" "I was thinking," said the postmaster, "of teaching you to read," and then for the rest of the afternoon, he taught her the alphabet.

Thus, in a very short time, Ratan had got as far as the double consonants.

It seemed as though the showers of the season would never end. Canals, ditches, and hollows were all overflowing with water. All day and night, the pattering of the rains and the croaking of frogs was heard. The village roads became impassable, and marketing had to be done in punts.

One heavily clouded morning, the postmaster's little pupil had been long waiting outside the door for her call, but, not hearing it, as usual, she took up her dog-eared book, and slowly entered the room. She found her master stretched out on his bed, and, thinking that he was resting, she was about to retire on tip-toe, when she suddenly heard her name—"Ratan!" She turned at once and asked, "Were you sleeping, Dada?" The postmaster in a plaintive voice said, "I am not well. Feel my head, is it very hot?"

In the loneliness of his exile, and in the gloom of the rains, his ailing body needed a little tender nursing. He longed to remember the touch on the forehead of soft hands with tinkling bracelets, to imagine the presence of loving womanhood, the nearness of mother and sister. But exile was not that disappointing. Ratan ceased to be a little girl. She at once stepped into the post of a mother, called in the village doctor, gave the patient his pills at the proper intervals, sat up all night by his pillow, cooked his gruel for him, and every now and then asked, "Are you feeling a little better, Dada?"

It was sometime before the postmaster, with a weakened body, was able to leave his sick-bed. "No more of this," said he with the decision, "I must get a transfer." He at once wrote off to Calcutta an application for a transfer, on the ground of the unhealthiness of the place.

Relieved from her duties as a nurse, Ratan again took up her old place outside the door. But she no longer heard the same old call. She would sometimes peep inside furtively to find the postmaster sitting on his chair, or stretched on his bed, and staring absent-mindedly into the air. While Ratan was awaiting her call, the postmaster was awaiting a reply to his application. The girl read her old lessons over and over again. Her great fear was lest, when the call came, she might be found wanting in the double consonants. At last, after a week, the call did come one evening. With an overflowing heart, Ratan rushed into the room and said, "Were you calling me, Dada?"

The postmaster said, "I am going away to-morrow, Ratan."

"Where are you going, Dada?"

"I am going home."

"When will you come back?"

"I am not coming back."

Ratan asked no other question. The postmaster, of his own accord, went on to tell her that his application for a transfer had been rejected, so he had resigned his post and was going home.

For a long time, neither of them spoke another word. The lamp went on dimly burning, and from a leak in one corner of the thatch water dripped steadily into an earthen vessel on the floor beneath it.

After a while, Ratan rose and went off to the kitchen to prepare the meal, but she was not as quick about it as on other days. Many new things to think of had entered her little brain. When the postmaster had finished his supper, the girl suddenly asked him, "Dada, will you take me to your home?"

The postmaster laughed. "What an idea!" said he, but he did not think it necessary to explain to the girl wherein lay the absurdity.

That whole night, in her waking and in her dreams, the postmaster's laughing reply haunted her, "What an idea!"

On getting up in the morning, the postmaster found his bath ready. He had stuck to his Calcutta habit of bathing in water drawn and kept in pitchers, instead of taking a plunge in the river as was the custom of the village. For some reason or other, the girl could not ask him about the time of his departure, so she had fetched the water from the river long before sunrise that he would be ready as early as he might want it. After the bath, he called Ratan. She entered noiselessly and looked silently into her master's face for orders. The master said, "You need not be anxious about my going away, Ratan, I shall tell my successor to look after you." These words were kindly meant, no doubt, but inscrutable are the ways of a woman's heart!

Ratan had borne many a scolding from her master without complaint, but these kind words she could not bear. She burst out weeping, and said, "No, no, you need not tell anybody anything at all about me, I don't want to stay on here."

The postmaster was dumbfounded. He had never seen Ratan like this before.

The new incumbent duly arrived, and the postmaster, having given overcharge, prepared to depart. Just before starting he called Ratan and said, "Here is something for you, I hope it will keep you for some little time." He brought out from his pocket the whole of his month's salary, retaining only a trifle for his travelling expenses. Then Ratan fell at his feet and cried, "Oh, Dada, I pray you, don't give me anything, don't in any way trouble about me," and then she ran away out of sight.

The postmaster heaved a sigh, took up his carpet bag, put his umbrella over his shoulder, and, accompanied by a man carrying his many-coloured tin trunk, he slowly made for the boat.

When he got in and the boat was underway, and the rain-swollen river, like a stream of tears welling up from the earth, swirled and sobbed at her bows, then he felt a pain at heart, the grief-stricken face of a village girl seemed to represent for him the great unspoken pervading grief of Mother Earth herself.

At one time he had an impulse to go back and bring away along with him that lonesome waif, forsaken of the world. But the wind had just filled the sails, the boat had got well into the middle of the turbulent current, and already the village was left behind, and its outlying burning-ground came in sight.

So the traveller, borne on the breast of the swift-flowing river, consoled himself with philosophical reflections on the numberless meetings and partings going on in the world—on death, the great parting, from which none returns.

But Ratan had no philosophy. She was wandering about the post office in a flood of tears. It may be that she had still a lurking hope in some corner of her heart that her Dada would return, and that is why she could not tear herself away. Alas for our foolish human nature! Its fond mistakes are persistent. The dictates of reason take a long time to assert their own sway. The surest proofs meanwhile are disbelieved. False hope is clung to with all one's might and main, till a day comes when it has sucked the heart dry and it forcibly breaks through its bonds and departs. After that comes the misery of awakening, and then once again the longing to get back into the maze of the same mistakes.

6
Master Mashai

I

Adhar Babu lives upon the interest of the capital left to him by his father. Only the brokers, negotiating loans, come to his drawing room and smoke the silver-chased hookah, and the clerks from the attorney's office discuss the terms of some mortgage or the amount of the stamp fees. He is so careful with his money that even the most dogged efforts of the boys from the local football club fail to make any impression on his pocket.

At the time this story opens and a new guest comes into his household. After a long period of despair, his wife, Nanibala, bore him a son.

The child resembled his mother, with large eyes, a well-formed nose, and fair complexion. Ratikanta, Adharlal's protégé, gave verdict that, "he is worthy of this noble house" and they named him Venugopal.

Never before had Adharlal's wife expressed any opinion differing from her husband's on household expenses. There had been a discussion now and then about the propriety of some necessary item and up to this time she had merely acknowledged defeat with silent contempt. But now Adharlal could no longer maintain his supremacy. He had to give way little by little when things for his son were in question.

II

As Venugopal grew up, his father gradually became accustomed to spending money on him. He obtained an old teacher, who had a considerable repute for his learning and also for his success in dragging impassable boys through their examinations. But such training does not lead to the cultivation of amiability. This man tried his best to win the boy's heart, but the little kindness that was left in him had turned sour, and the child repulsed his advances from the very beginning. The mother, in consequence, objected to him strongly, and complained that the very sight of him made her boy ill. So the teacher left.

Just then, Haralal made his appearance with a dirty dress and a torn pair of old canvas shoes. Haralal's mother, who was a widow, had kept him with great difficulty at a District school out of the scanty earnings which she made by cooking in strange houses and husking rice. He managed to pass the matriculation and determined to go to college. As a result of his half-starved condition, his pinched face tapered to a point in an unnatural manner like Cape Comorin in the map of India, and the only broad portion of it was his forehead, which resembled the ranges of the Himalayas.

The servant asked Haralal what he wanted, and he answered timidly that he wished to see the master.

The servant answered sharply, "You can't see him." Haralal was hesitating, at a loss what to do next, when Venugopal, who had finished his game in the garden, suddenly came to the door. The servant shouted at Haralal, "Get away." Quite unaccountably Venugopal grew excited and cried, "No, he shan't get away." And he dragged the stranger to his father.

Adharlal had just risen from his mid-day sleep and was sitting quietly on the upper verandah in his cane chair, rocking his legs.

Ratikanta was enjoying his hookah, seated in a chair next to him. He asked Haralal how far he had got in his reading. The young man bent his head and answered that he has passed the matriculation. Ratikanta looked stern and expressed surprise that he should be so backward for his age. Haralal kept silence. It was Ratikanta's special pleasure to torture his patron's dependants, whether actual or potential.

Suddenly it struck Adharlal that he would be able to employ this youth as a tutor for his son on next to nothing. He agreed, then and there to take him at a salary of five rupees a month with board and lodging free.

III

This time, the post of tutor remained occupied longer than before. From the very beginning of their acquaintance Haralal and his pupil became great friends. Never before did Haralal have such an opportunity of loving any young child. His mother had been so poor and dependent, that he had never had the privilege of playing with the children where she was employed at work. He had not hitherto suspected the hidden stores of love which lay all the while accumulating in his own heart.

Venu, also, was glad to find a companion in Haralal. He was the only boy in the house. His two younger sisters were looked down upon, as unworthy of being his playmates. So his new tutor became his only companion, patiently bearing the undivided weight of the tyranny of his child friend.

IV

Venu was now eleven. Haralal had passed his intermediate, winning a scholarship. He was working hard for his B.A. degree. After college lectures were over, he would take Venu out into the public park and tell him stories about the heroes from Greek History and Victor Hugo's romances. The child used to get quite impatient to run to Haralal, after school hours, in spite of his mother's attempts to keep him by her side.

This displeased Nanibala. She thought that it was a deep-laid plot of Haralal's to captivate her boy, in order to prolong his own appointment. One day, she talked to him from behind the purdah, "It is your duty to teach my son only for an hour or two in the morning and evening. But why are you always with him? The child has nearly forgotten his own parents. You must understand that a man of your position is no fit companion for a boy belonging to this house."

Haralal's voice choked a little as he answered that for the future he would merely be Venu's teacher and would keep away from him at other times.

It was Haralal's usual practice to begin his college study early before dawn. The child would come to him directly after he had washed himself. There was a small pool in the garden and they used to feed the fish in it with puffed rice. Venu also engaged in building a miniature garden-house, at the corner of the garden, with its liliputian gates and hedges and gravel paths. When the sun became too hot they would go back into the house, and Venu would have his morning lesson from Haralal.

On the day in question, Venu had risen earlier than usual, because he wished to hear the end of the story which Haralal had begun the evening before. But he found his teacher absent. When asked about him, the door-servant said that he had gone out. At lesson time, Venu remained unnaturally quiet. He never even asked Haralal why he had gone out, but went on mechanically with his lessons. When the child was with his mother taking his breakfast, she asked him what had happened to make him so gloomy, and why he was not taking his meals on time. Venu gave no answer. After his meal, his mother caressed him and questioned him repeatedly. Venu burst out crying and said, "Master Mashai!" His mother asked Venu, "What about Master Mashai?" But Venu found it difficult to name the offence which his teacher had committed.

His mother said to Venu, "Has your Master Mashai been saying anything to you against me?"

Venu could not understand the question and went away.

V

There was a theft in Adhar Babu's house. The police were called in to investigate. Even Haralal's trunks were searched. Ratikanta said, "The man who steals anything, does not keep his thefts in his own box."

Adharlal called his son's tutor and said to him, "It won't be convenient for me to keep any of you in my own house. From today you will have to take up your quarters outside, only coming in to teach my son at the proper time."

Drawing at his hookah, Ratikanta said, "That is a good proposal, beneficial for both parties."

Haralal did not utter a word, but he sent a letter saying that it would be no longer possible for him to remain as tutor to Venu.

When Venu came back from school, he found his tutor's room empty. Even that broken steel trunk of his was absent. The rope was stretched across the corner, but there were no clothes or towel hanging on it. Only on the table, which formerly was strewn with books and papers, stood a bowl containing some gold-fish with a label on which was written the word 'Venu' in Haralal's handwriting. The boy ran up at once to his father and asked him what had happened. His father told him that Haralal had resigned from his post. Venu went to his room and flung himself down and began to cry. Adharlal did not know what to do with him.

The next day, when Haralal was sitting on his wooden bedstead in the hostel, debating with himself whether he should attend his college lectures, suddenly he saw Adhar Babu's servant coming into his room followed by Venu. Venu at once ran up to him and threw his arms round his neck asking him to come back to the house.

Haralal could not explain why it was absolutely impossible for him to go back, but the memory of those clinging arms and that pathetic request used to choke his breath with emotion long after.

VI

Haralal found out, that his mind was in an unsettled state. He realized that he had but a small chance of winning the scholarship, even if he could pass the examination. At the same time, he knew that, without the scholarship, he would not be able to continue his studies. So he tried to get employment in some office.

Fortunately for him, an English Manager of a big merchant firm took a fancy to him at first sight. After only a brief exchange of words the Manager asked him if he had any experience, and could he bring any testimonial. Haralal could only answer, "No." Nevertheless, a post was offered him of twenty rupees a month and fifteen rupees were allowed him in advance to help him to come properly dressed to the office.

The Manager made Haralal work extremely hard. He had to stay on after office hours and sometimes go to his master's house late in the evening. But, in this way, he learnt his work quicker than others, and his fellow clerks became jealous of him and tried to injure him, but without effect. He rented a small house in a narrow lane and brought his mother to live with him as soon as his salary was raised to forty rupees a month. Thus happiness came back to his mother after weary years of waiting.

Haralal's mother used to express a desire to see Venugopal, of whom she had heard so much. She prepared some dishes and asked him to come, atleast once, to dine with her son. Haralal avoided the subject by saying that his house was not big enough to invite him for that purpose.

VII

The news reached Haralal that Venu's mother had died. He could not wait a moment, but went at once to Adharlal's house to see Venu. After that, they began to see each other frequently.

But times had changed. Venu, stroking his budding moustache, had grown quite a young man of fashion. Friends, befitting his present condition, were numerous. That old dilapidated study chair and ink-stained desk had vanished, and the room now seemed to be bursting with pride at its new acquisitions, its looking-glasses, oleographs, and other furniture. Venu had entered college, but showed no haste in crossing the boundary of the intermediate examination.

Haralal remembered his mother's request to invite Venu to dinner. After great hesitation, he did so. Venugopal, with his handsome face, at once won the mother's heart. But as soon as ever the meal was over he became impatient to go, and looking at his gold watch he explained that he had pressing engagements elsewhere. Then he jumped into his carriage, which was waiting at the door and drove away. Haralal with a sigh said to himself that he would never invite him again.

VIII

One day, on returning from office, Haralal noticed the presence of a man in his house. Possibly he would have passed him by, had not the heavy scent of some foreign perfume attracted his attention. Haralal asked who was there, and the answer came, "It is I, Master Mashai."

"What is the matter, Venu?" said Haralal, "When did you arrive?"

"I came hours ago," said Venu, "I did not know that you returned so late."

They went upstairs together and Haralal lighted the lamp and asked Venu whether all was well. Venu replied that his college classes were becoming a fearful bore, and his father did not realize how dreadfully hard it was for him to go on in the same class, year after year, with students much younger than himself. Haralal asked him what he wished to do. Venu then told him that he wanted to go to England and become a barrister. He gave an instance of a student, much less advanced than him, who was getting ready to go. Haralal asked him if he had received his father's permission. Venu replied that his father would not hear a word of it until he had passed the Intermediate, and that was impossible in his present frame of mind. Haralal suggested that he himself should go and try to talk over his father.

"No," said Venu, "I can never allow that!"

Haralal asked Venu to stay for dinner. While they were waiting, he gently placed his hand on Venu's shoulder and said, "Venu, you should not quarrel with your father, or leave home."

Venu jumped up angrily and said that if he was not welcome, he could go elsewhere. Haralal caught him by the hand and implored him not to go away without taking his food. But Venu snatched away his hand and was just leaving the room when Haralal's mother brought the food in on a tray. On seeing Venu about to leave she pressed him to remain.

While he was eating the sound of a carriage stopping at the door was heard. First a servant entered the room with creaking shoes and then Adhar Babu himself. Venu's face became pale. The mother left the room as soon as she saw strangers enter. Adhar Babu called out to Haralal in a voice thick with anger, "Ratikanta gave me full warning, but I could not believe that you had such devilish cunning hidden in you. So, you think you're going to live upon Venu? This is sheer kidnapping, and I shall prosecute you in the Police Court."

Venu silently followed his father and went out of the house.

IX

The firm to which Haralal belonged began to buy up large quantities of rice and dal from the country districts. To pay for this, Haralal had to take the cash every Saturday morning by the early train and disburse it. There were special centres where the brokers and middlemen would come with their receipts and accounts for settlement. Some discussion had taken place in the office about Haralal being entrusted with this work, without any security, but the manager undertook all the responsibility and said that a security was not needed. This special work used to go on from the middle of December to the middle of April. Haralal would get back from it very late at night.

One day, after his return, he was told by his mother that Venu had called and that she had persuaded him to take his dinner at their house. This happened more than once. The mother said that it was because Venu missed his own mother, and the tears came into her eyes as she spoke about it.

One day, Venu waited for Haralal to return and had a long talk with him.

"Master Mashai!" he said, "Father has become so cantankerous lately that I cannot live with him any longer. And, besides, I know that he is getting ready to marry again. Ratikanta is seeking a suitable match, and they are always conspiring about it. There used to be a time when my father would get anxious, if I was absent from home even for a few hours. Now, if I am away for more than a week, he takes no notice, infact he seems greatly relieved. If this marriage takes place, I feel that I cannot live in the house any longer. You must show me a way out of this. I want to become independent."

Haralal felt deeply pained, but he did not know how to help his former pupil. Venu said that he was determined to go to England and become a barrister. By hook or by crook, he has to get some money to go to England or he could borrow it on a note of hand and his father would have to pay when the creditors filed a suit. With this borrowed money he would get away and when he finally reaches England, his father shall certainly to remit his expenses.

"But who is there," Haralal asked, "who would advance you the money?"

"You!" said Venu.

"I!" exclaimed Haralal in amazement.

"Yes," said Venu, "I've seen the servant bringing heaps of money here in bags."

"The servant and the money belongs to someone else," explained Haralal.

Haralal explained why the money came to his house at night, so that it would be scattered next morning.

"But can't the manager advance the sum?" Venu asked.

"He may do so," said Haralal, "if your father stands security."

The discussion ended at this point.

X

One Friday night, a carriage and pair stopped before Haralal's lodging house. When Venu was announced Haralal was counting money in his bedroom, seated on the floor. Venu entered wearing a Parsee coat and trousers and had a cap on his head. Rings were prominent on almost all the fingers of both hands, and a thick gold chain was hanging round his neck, there was a gold-watch in his pocket, and diamond studs could be seen peeping from his shirt sleeves. Haralal at once asked him what the matter was and why he was wearing that dress.

"My father's marriage," said Venu, "comes off tomorrow. He tried hard to keep it from me, but I found it out. I asked him to allow me to go to our garden-house at Barrackpur for a few days, and he was only too glad to get rid of me so easily. I am going there, and I wish to God never to come back."

Haralal looked pointedly at the rings on his fingers. Venu explained that they belonged to his mother. Haralal then asked him if he had already had his dinner. He answered, "Yes, haven't you had yours?"

"No," said Haralal, "I cannot leave this room until I have all the money safely locked up in this iron chest."

"Go and take your dinner," said Venu, "while I keep guard here. Your mother is waiting for you."

For a moment Haralal hesitated, and then he went out and had his dinner. In a short time, he came back with his mother and the three of them sat among the bags of money talking together. When it was about midnight, Venu took out his watch and looked at it and jumped up saying that he would miss his train. Then he asked Haralal to keep all his rings and his watch and chain until he asked for them again. Haralal put them all together in a leather bag and laid it in the iron safe. Venu went out.

The canvas bags containing the currency notes had already been placed in the safe, only the loose coins remained to be counted over and put away with the rest.

XI

Haralal lay down on the floor of the same room, with the key under his pillow, and went to sleep. He dreamt that Venu's mother was loudly reproaching him from behind the curtain. Her words were indistinct, but rays of different colours from the jewels on her body kept piercing the curtain like needles and violently vibrating. Haralal struggled to call Venu, but his voice seemed to forsake him. At last, with a noise, the curtain fell down. Haralal started up from his sleep and found darkness piled up round about him. A sudden gust of wind had flung open the window and put out the light. Haralal's whole body was wet with perspiration. He relighted the lamp and saw, by the clock, that it was four in the morning. There was no time to sleep again, for he had to get ready to start.

After Haralal had washed his face and hands his mother called from her own room, "Baba, why are you up so soon?"

It was the habit of Haralal to see his mother's face the first thing in the morning in order to bring a blessing upon the day. His mother said to him, "I was dreaming that you were going out to bring back a bride for yourself." Haralal went to his own bedroom and began to take out the bags containing the silver and the currency notes.

Suddenly his heart stopped beating. Three of the bags appeared to be empty. He knocked them against the iron safe, but this only proved his fear to be true. He opened them and shook them with all his might. Two letters from Venu dropped out from one of the bags. One was addressed to his father and one to Haralal.

Haralal tore open his own letter and began reading. The words seemed to run into one another. He trimmed the lamp, but felt as if he could not understand what he read. Yet the purport of the letter was clear. Venu had taken three thousand rupees, in currency notes, and had started for England. The steamer was to sail before day-break that very morning. The letter ended with the words, "I am explaining everything in a letter to my father. He will pay off the debt, and then, again, my mother's ornaments, which I have left in your care, will more than cover the amount I have taken."

Haralal locked up his room and hired a carriage and went with all haste to the jetty. But he did not know even the name of the steamer which Venu had taken. He ran the whole length of the wharves from Prinsep's Ghat to Metiaburuj. He found that two steamers had started on their voyage to England early that morning. It was impossible for him to know which of them carried Venu, or how to reach him.

When Haralal got home, the sun was strong and the whole of Calcutta was awake. Everything before his eyes seemed blurred. He felt as if he were pushing against a fearful obstacle which was bodiless and without pity. His mother came on the verandah to ask him anxiously where he had gone. With a dry laugh he said to her, "To bring home a bride for myself!" and then he fainted away.

On opening his eyes after a while, Haralal asked his mother to leave him. Entering his room he shut the door from the inside while his mother remained seated on the floor of the verandah in the fierce glare of the sun. She kept calling to him fitfully, almost mechanically, "Baba, Baba!"

The servant came from the manager's office and knocked at the door, saying that they would miss the train if they did not start out at once. Haralal called from inside, "It will not be possible for me to start this morning."

"Then where are we to go, Sir?"

"I will tell you later on."

The servant went downstairs with a gesture of impatience.

Suddenly Haralal thought of the ornaments which Venu had left behind. Up till now he had completely forgotten about them, but with the thought came instant relief. He took the leather bag containing them, and also Venu's letter to his father, and left the house.

Before he reached Adharlal's house he could hear the bands playing for the wedding, yet on entering he could feel that there had been some disturbance. Haralal was told that there had been a theft the night before and one or two servants were suspected. Adhar Babu was sitting in the upper verandah flushed with anger and Ratikanta was smoking his hookah. Haralal said to Adhar Babu, "I have something private to tell you." Adharlal flared up, "I have no time now!" He was afraid that Haralal had come to borrow money or to ask his help. Ratikanta suggested that if there was any delicacy in making the request in his presence he would leave the place. Adharlal told him angrily to sit where he was. Then Haralal handed over the bag which Venu had left behind. Adharlal asked what was inside it and Haralal opened it and gave the contents into his hands.

Then Adhar Babu said with a sneer, "It's a paid business that you two have started, you and your former pupil! You were certain that the stolen property would be traced, and so you come along with it to me to claim a reward!"

Haralal presented the letter which Venu had written to his father. This only made Adharlal all the more furious.

"What's all this?" he shouted, "I'll call for the police! My son has not yet come of age, and you have smuggled him out of the country! I'll bet my soul you've lent him a few hundred rupees, and then taken a note of hand for three thousand! But I am not going to be bound by this!"

"I never advanced him any money at all," said Haralal.

"Then how did he find it?" said Adharlal, "Do you mean to tell me he broke open your safe and stole it?"

Haralal stood silent.

Ratikanta sarcastically remarked, "I don't believe this fellow ever set hands on as much as three thousand rupees in his life."

When Haralal left the house he seemed to have lost the power of dreading anything, or even of being anxious. His mind seemed to refuse to work. He entered the lane and saw a carriage waiting before his own lodging. For a moment he felt certain that it was Venu's. It was impossible to believe that his calamity could be so hopelessly final.

Haralal went up quickly, but found an English assistant from the firm sitting inside the carriage. The man came out when he saw Haralal and took him by the hand and asked him, "Why didn't you go out by train this morning?" The servant had told the manager his suspicions and he had sent this man to find out.

Haralal answered, "Notes to the amount of three thousand rupees are missing."

The man asked how that could have happened.

Haralal remained silent.

The man said to Haralal, "Let us go upstairs together and see where you keep your money." They went up to the room and counted the money and made a thorough search of the house.

When the mother saw this she could not contain herself any longer. She came out before the stranger and said, "Baba, what has happened?" He answered in broken Hindi that some money had been stolen.

"Stolen!" the mother cried, "Why! How could it be stolen? Who could do such a bastardly thing?" Haralal said to her, "Mother, don't say a word."

The man collected the remainder of the money and told Haralal to come with him to the manager. The mother barred the way and said, "Sir, where are you taking my son? I have brought him up, starving and straining to do honest work. My son would never touch money belonging to others."

The Englishman, not knowing Bengali, said, "*Achcha! Achcha!*" Haralal told his mother not to be anxious, he would explain it all to the manager and soon be back again. The mother entreated him with a distressed voice, "Baba, you haven't taken a morsel of food all morning." Haralal stepped into the carriage and drove away, and the mother sank to the ground in the anguish of her heart.

The manager said to Haralal, "Tell me the truth. What actually happened?"

Haralal said to him, "I haven't taken any money."

"I fully believe it," said the manager, "but surely you know who has taken it."

Haralal looked on the ground and remained silent.

"Somebody," said the manager, "must have taken it away with your connivance."

"Nobody," replied Haralal, "could take it away with my knowledge without taking first my life."

"Look here, Haralal," said the Manager, "I trusted you completely. I took no security. I employed you in a post of great responsibility. Everyone in the office was against me for doing so.

Losing three thousand rupees is a small matter, but the shame of all this to me is a great matter. I will do one thing. I will give you the whole day to bring back this money. If you do so, I shall say nothing about it and I will keep you in your post."

It was now eleven o' clock. Haralal went out of the office. The clerks began to discuss the affair with exultation.

"What can I do? What can I do?" Haralal repeated to himself, as he walked along like one dazed, the sun's heat pouring down upon him. At last his mind ceased to think at all about what could be done, but the mechanical walk went on without ceasing.

This city of Calcutta, which offered its shelter to thousands and thousands of men had become like a steel trap. He could see no way out. The whole body of people were conspiring to surround and hold him captive, this most insignificant of men, whom no one knew. Nobody had any special grudge against him, yet everybody was his enemy. The crowd passed by, brushing against him, the clerks of the offices were eating their lunch on the road side from their plates made of leaves, a tired wayfarer on the *Maidan*, under the shade of a tree, was lying with one hand beneath his head and one leg upraised over the other. The up-country women, crowded into hackney carriages, were wending their way to the temple, a *chuprassie* came up with a letter and asked him the address on the envelope, so the afternoon went by.

Then came the time when the offices were all about to close. Carriages started off in all directions, carrying people back to their homes. The clerks, packed tightly on the seats of the trams, looked at the theatre advertisements as they returned to their lodgings. From today, Haralal had neither his work in the office, nor release from work in the evening. He had no need to hurry to catch the tram to take him to his home.

All the busy occupations of the city-the buildings-the horses and carriages-the incessant traffic-seemed, now at one time, to swell into dreadful reality, and at another time, to subside into the shadowy unreal.

Haralal had taken neither food, nor rest, nor shelter all that day.

The street lamps were lighted from one road to another and it seemed to him that a watchful darkness, like some demon, was keeping its eyes wide open to guard every movement of its victim. Haralal did not even have the energy to enquire how late it was. The veins on his forehead throbbed, and he felt as if his head would burst. Through the paroxysms of pain, which alternated with the apathy of dejection, only one thought came again and again to his mind, among the innumerable multitudes in that vast city, only one name found its way through his dry throat, "Mother!"

He said to himself, "At the deep of night, when no one is awake to capture me, I will silently creep to my mother's arms and fall asleep, never to wake again!"

Haralal's one trouble was lest some police officer should molest him in the presence of his mother, and this kept him back from going home. When it became impossible for him at last to bear the weight of his own body, he hailed a carriage. The driver asked him where he wanted to go. He said, "Nowhere. I want you to drive across the *Maidan* to get some fresh air." The man at first did not believe him and was about to drive on, when Haralal put a rupee into his hand as an advance payment. Thereupon the driver crossed, and then re-crossed, the *Maidan* from one side to the other, traversing different roads.

Haralal laid his throbbing head on the side of the open window of the carriage and closed his eyes. Slowly all the pain abated. His body became cool. A deep and intense peace filled his heart and a supreme deliverance seemed to embrace him on every side. It was not the day's despair that threatened him with its grip of utter helplessness, but only an empty fear of the mind. Deliverance was in the infinite sky and there was no end to peace. No king or emperor in the world had the power to keep captive this nonentity, this Haralal. In the sky, surrounding his emancipated heart on every side, he felt the presence of his mother, that one poor woman. She seemed to grow and grow till she filled the infinity of darkness. All the roads and buildings and shops of Calcutta gradually became enveloped by her. In her presence vanished all the aching pains and thoughts and consciousness of Haralal. It burst that bubble filled with the hot vapour of pain. And now there was neither darkness nor light, but only tense fullness.

The Cathedral clock struck one. The driver called out impatiently, "Babu, my horse can't go on any longer. Where do you want to go?"

There came no answer.

The driver came down and shook Haralal and asked him again where he wanted to go.

There came no answer.

And the answer was never received from Haralal, where he wanted to go.

7
Subha

When the girl was given the name of Subhashini, who could have guessed that she would prove dumb? Her two elder sisters were Sukeshini and Suhasini, and for the sake of uniformity her father named his youngest girl Subhashini. Everyone called her Subha.

Her two elder sisters had been married with the usual cost and difficulty, and now the youngest daughter lay like a silent weight upon the heart of her parents. The entire world seemed to think that, because she did not speak, therefore she did not feel. It discussed her future and its own anxiety freely in her presence. She had understood from her earliest childhood that God had sent her like a curse to her father's house, so she withdrew herself from ordinary people and tried to live apart. If only they would all forget her she felt she could endure it. But who can forget pain? Night and day her parents' minds ached on her account. Especially her mother looked upon her as a deformity in herself. To a mother a daughter is a more closely intimate part of herself than a son can be, and a fault in her is a source of personal shame. Banikantha, Subha's father, loved her rather better than his other daughters, her mother regarded her with aversion as a stain upon her own body.

If Subha lacked speech, she did not lack a pair of large dark eyes, shaded with long lashes, and her lips trembled like a leaf in response to any thought that rose in her mind.

When we express our thought in words, the medium is not found easily. There must be a process of translation, which is often inexact, and then it became erroneous. But black eyes need no translating, the mind itself throws a shadow upon them. In them thought opens or shuts, shines forth or goes out in darkness, hangs steadfast like the setting moon or like the swift and restless lightning illumines all quarters of the sky. They, who from birth have had no other speech than the trembling of their lips, learn the language of the eyes, endless in expression, deep as the sea, clear as the heavens, wherein play dawn and sunset, light and shadow. The dumb have a lonely grandeur like Nature's own. Wherefore the other children almost dreaded Subha and never played with her. She was silent and companionless as noontide.

The hamlet where she lived was Chandipur. Its river, small for a river of Bengal, kept to its narrow bounds like a daughter of the middle class. This busy streak of water never overflowed its banks, but went about its duties as though it were a member of every family in the villages beside it. On either side were houses and banks shaded with trees. So stepping from her queenly throne, the river goddess became a garden deity of each home, and forgetful of herself performed her task of endless benediction with swift and cheerful foot.

Banikantha's house looked out upon the stream. Every hut and stack in the place could be seen by the passing boatmen. I know not if amid these signs of worldly wealth anyone noticed the little girl who, when her work was done, stole away to the waterside and sat there. But here nature fulfilled her want of speech and spoke for her. The murmur of the brook, the voice of the village folk, the songs of the boatmen, the crying of the birds and rustle of trees mingled and were one with the trembling of her heart. They became one vast wave of sound which beat upon her restless soul. This murmur and movement of nature were the dumb girl's language, that speech of the dark eyes, which the long lashes shaded, was the language of the world about her. From the trees, where the cicalas chirped, to the quiet stars there was nothing but signs and gestures, weeping and sighing. And in the deep mid-noon, when the boatmen and fisher-folk had gone to their dinner, when the villagers slept and birds were still, when the ferry-boats were idle, when the great busy world paused in its toil and became suddenly a lonely, awful giant, then beneath the vast impressive heavens there were only dumb nature and a dumb girl, sitting silently, one under the spreading sunlight, the other where a small tree cast its shadow.

But Subha was not altogether without friends. In the stall were two cows, Sarbbashi and Panguli. They had never heard their names from her lips, but they knew her footfall. Though she had no words, she murmured lovingly and they understood her gentle murmuring better than all speech. When she fondled them or scolded or coaxed them, they understood her better than men could do. Subha would come to the shed and throw her arms round Sarbbashi's neck, she would rub her cheek against her friend's, and Panguli would turn her great kind eyes and lick her face. The girl paid them three regular visits every day and others that were irregular. Whenever she heard any words that hurt her, she would come to these dumb friends out of due time. It was as though they guessed her anguish of spirit from her quiet look of sadness. Coming close to her, they would rub their horns softly against her arms, and in dumb, puzzled fashion try to comfort her. Besides these two, there were goats and a kitten, but Subha had not the same equality of friendship with them, though they showed the same attachment. Every time it got a chance, night or day, the kitten would jump into her lap, and settle down to slumber, and show its appreciation of an aid to sleep as Subha drew her soft fingers over its neck and back.

Subha also had a comrade among the higher animals, and it is hard to say what kind of friendship they shared, for he could speak, and his gift of speech left them without any common language. He was the youngest boy of the Gosains, Pratap by name, and an idle fellow. After long effort, his parents had abandoned the hope that he would ever make his living. Now losels have this advantage, that, though their own folk disapprove of them, they are generally popular with everyone else. Having no work to chain them, they become public property. Just as every town needs an open space where all may breathe, so a village needs two or three gentlemen of leisure, who can give time to all, then, if we are lazy and want a companion, one is to hand.

Pratap's chief ambition was to catch fish. He managed to waste a lot of time this way, and might be seen almost any afternoon so employed. It was thus most often that he met Subha. Whatever he was about, he liked a companion, and, when one is catching fish, a silent companion is best of all. Pratap respected Subha for her taciturnity, and, as every one called her Subha, he showed his affection by calling her 'Su'. Subha used to sit beneath a tamarind, and Pratap, a little distance off, would cast his line. Pratap took with him a small allowance of betel, and Subha prepared it for him. And I think that, sitting and gazing a long while, she desired ardently to bring some great help to Pratap, to be of real aid, to prove by any means that she was not a useless burden to the world. But there was nothing to do. Then she turned to the Creator in prayer for some rare power, that by an astonishing miracle she might startle Pratap into exclaiming, "My! I never dreamt our Su could have done this!"

If Subha would have been a water nymph, she might have risen slowly from the river, bringing the gem of a snake's crown to the landing-place. Then Pratap, leaving his paltry fishing, might dive into the lower world, and see there, on a golden bed in a palace of silver, whom else but dumb little Su, Banikantha's child? Yes, our Su, the only daughter of the king of that shining city of jewels! But it was impossible. Not that anything is really impossible, but Su had been born, not into the royal house of Patalpur, but into Banikantha's family, and she knew no means of astonishing the Gosains' boy.

When she grew up, gradually she began to find herself. A new inexpressible consciousness like a tide from the central places of the sea, when the moon is full, swept through her. She saw herself, questioned herself, but no answer came that she could understand.

One night, she slowly opened her door and peeped out timidly. Nature, herself at full moon, like lonely Subha, was looking down on the sleeping earth. Her strong young life beat within her, joy and sadness filled her being to its brim, she reached the limits even of her own illimitable loneliness, nay, passed beyond them. Her heart was heavy, and she could not speak. At the skirts of this silent troubled mother there stood a silent troubled girl.

The thought of her marriage filled her parents with anxious care. People blamed them, and even talked of making them outcasts. Banikantha was well off, they had fish-curry twice daily, and consequently he did not lack enemies. Then the women interfered, and Bani went away for a few days. Presently he returned and said, "We must go to Calcutta."

They got ready to go to this strange country. Subha's heart was heavy with tears, like a mist-wrapt dawn. With a vague fear that had been gathering for days, she dogged her father and mother like a dumb animal. With her large eyes wide open, she scanned their faces as though she wished to learn something. But not a word did they vouchsafe. One afternoon in the midst of all this, as Pratap was fishing, he laughed, "So, Su, they have caught your bridegroom, and you are going to be married! Mind you don't forget me altogether!" Then he turned his mind again to his fish. Just like a stricken doe looks in the hunter's face, asking in silent agony, "What have I done to you?" so did Subha looked at Pratap. That day, she sat no longer beneath her tree. Banikantha, having finished his nap, was smoking in his bedroom when Subha dropped down at his feet and burst out weeping as she gazed towards him. Banikantha tried to comfort her, and his cheek was wet with tears.

It was settled that the next day, they would go to Calcutta. Subha went to the cowshed to bid farewell to her childhood's comrades. She fed them with her hand, clasped their necks, looked into their faces, and tears fell fast from the eyes which spoke for her. That night was the tenth of the moon. Subha left her room, and flung herself down on her grassy couch beside her dear river. It was as if she threw her hands around, her strong silent mother, and tried to say, "Do not let me leave you, mother. Put your arms about me, as I have put mine about you, and hold me fast."

One day in a house in Calcutta, Subha's mother dressed her up with great care. She imprisoned her hair, knotting it up in laces, she hung her about with ornaments, and did her best to kill her natural beauty. Subha's eyes filled with tears. Her mother, fearing they would grow swollen with weeping, scolded her harshly, but the tears disregarded the scolding. The bridegroom came with a friend to inspect the bride. Her parents were dizzy with anxiety and fear when they saw the arrival of the God to select the beast for his sacrifice. Behind the stage, the mother called her instructions aloud, and increased her daughter's weeping twofold, before she sent her into the examiner's presence. The great man, after scanning her for a long time, said, "Not so bad."

He took special note of her tears, and thought she must have a tender heart. He put it to her credit in the account, arguing that the heart, which today was distressed at leaving her parents, would presently prove a useful possession. Like the oyster's pearls, the child's tears only increased her value, and he made no other comment.

The almanac was consulted, and the marriage took place on an auspicious day. Having delivered over their dumb girl into another's hands, Subha's parents returned home. Thank God! Their caste in this and their safety in the next world were assured! The bridegroom's work lay in the west, and shortly after the marriage he took his wife thither.

In less than ten days everyone knew that the bride was dumb! At least, if any one did not, it was not her fault, for she deceived no one. Her eyes told them everything, though no one understood her. She looked on every hand, she found no speech, and she missed the faces, familiar from birth, of those who had understood a dumb girl's language. In her silent heart there sounded an endless, voiceless weeping, which only the Searcher of Hearts could hear.

8
The Castaway

Towards evening the storm was at its height. From the terrific downpour of rain, the crash of thunder, and the repeated flashes of lightning, you might think that a battle of the gods and demons was raging in the skies. Black clouds waved like the flags of doom. The Ganges was lashed into a fury, and the trees of the gardens on either bank swayed from side to side with sighs and groans.

In a closed room of one of the riverside houses at Chandernagore, a husband and his wife were seated on a bed spread on the floor, intently discussing. An earthen lamp burned beside them.

The husband, Sharat, was saying, "I wish you would stay on a few days more, you would then be able to return home quite strong again."

The wife, Kiran, was saying, "I have quite recovered already. It will not, cannot possibly, do me any harm to go home now."

Every married person will at once understand that the conversation was not quite so brief as I have reported it. The matter was not difficult, but the arguments for and against did not advance it towards a solution. Like a rudderless boat, the discussion kept turning round and round the same point, and at last threatened to be overwhelmed in a flood of tears.

Sharat said, "The doctor thinks you should stop here a few days longer."

Kiran replied, "Your doctor knows everything!"

"Well," said Sharat, "you know that just now all sorts of illnesses are abroad. You would do well to stop here a month or two more."

"And at this moment, I suppose everyone in this place is perfectly well!"

What had happened was this, Kiran was a universal favourite with her family and neighbours, so that, when she fell seriously ill, they were all anxious. The village wiseacres thought it shameless for her husband to make so much fuss about a mere wife and even to suggest a change of air, and asked if Sharat supposed that no woman had ever been ill before, or whether he had found out that the folk of the place to which he meant to take her were immortal. Did he imagine that the writ of Fate did not run there? But Sharat and his mother turned a deaf ear to them, thinking that the little life of their darling was of greater importance than the united wisdom of a village. People are wont to reason thus when danger threatens their loved ones. So Sharat went to Chandernagore, and Kiran recovered, though she was still very weak. There was a pinched look on her face which filled the beholder with pity, and made his heart tremble, as he thought how narrowly she had escaped death.

Kiran was fond of society and amusement, the loneliness of her riverside villa did not suit her at all. There was nothing to do, there were no interesting neighbours, and she hated to be busy all day with medicine and dieting. There was no fun in measuring doses and making fomentations. Such was the subject discussed in their closed room on this stormy evening.

So long as Kiran deigned to argue, there was a chance of a fair fight. When she ceased to reply, and with a toss of her head disconsolately looked the other way, the poor man was disarmed. He was on the point of surrendering unconditionally when a servant shouted a message through the shut door.

Sharat got up. On opening the door, he learnt that a boat had been upset in the storm, and one of the occupants, a young Brahmin boy, had succeeded in swimming ashore at their garden.

Kiran was at once her own sweet self and set to work to get out some dry clothes for the boy. She then warmed a cup of milk and invited him to her room.

The boy had long curly hair, big expressive eyes, and no sign yet of hair on the face. Kiran, after getting him to drink some milk asked him all about himself.

He told her that his name was Nilkanta, and that he belonged to a theatrical troupe. They were coming to play in a neighbouring villa when the boat had suddenly foundered in the storm. He had no idea what had become of his companions. He was a good swimmer and had just managed to reach the shore.

The boy stayed with them. His narrow escape from a terrible death made Kiran take a warm interest in him. Sharat thought the boy's appearance at this moment rather a good thing, as his wife would now have something to amuse her, and might be persuaded to stay on for some time longer. Her mother-in-law, too, was pleased at the prospect of profiting their Brahmin guest by her kindness. And Nilkanta himself was delighted at his double escape from his master and from the other world, as well as at finding a home in this wealthy family.

In a short while, Sharat and his mother changed their opinion, and longed for his departure. The boy found a secret pleasure in smoking Sharat's hookahs, he would calmly go off in pouring rain with Sharat's best silk umbrella for a stroll through the village, and make friends with all whom he met. Moreover, he had got hold of a mongrel village dog which he petted so recklessly that it came indoors with muddy paws, and left tokens of its visit on Sharat's spotless bed. Then he gathered about him a devoted band of boys of all sorts and sizes, and the result was that not a solitary mango in the neighbourhood had a chance of ripening that season.

There is no doubt that Kiran had a hand in spoiling the boy. Sharat often warned her about it, but she would not listen to him. She made a dandy of him with Sharat's cast-off clothes, and gave him new ones also. She was intently drawn towards hm, had developed a curiosity to know more about him and she constantly called him to her own room. After her bath and midday meal, Kiran would be seated on the bedstead with her betel-leaf box by her side. While her maid combed and dried her hair, Nilkanta would stand in front and recite pieces out of his repertory with appropriate gesture and song, his elf-locks waving wildly. Thus, the long afternoon hours passed merrily away. Kiran would often try to persuade Sharat to sit with her as one of the audience, but Sharat, who had taken a cordial dislike to the boy, refused, nor could Nilkanta do his part half so well when Sharat was there. His mother would sometimes be lured by the hope of hearing sacred names in the recitation, but love of her mid-day sleep speedily overcame devotion, and she lay lapped in dreams.

The boy often got his ears boxed and pulled by Sharat, but as this was nothing to what he had been used to as a member of the troupe, he did not mind it in the least. In his short experience of the world, he had come to the conclusion that, as the earth consisted of land and water, so human life was made up of eatings and beatings, and that the beatings largely predominated.

It was hard to tell Nilkanta's age. If it was about fourteen or fifteen, then his face was too old for his years, if seventeen or eighteen, then he was too young. He was either a man too early or a boy too late. Joining the theatrical band at a very young age, he had played the parts of Radhika, Damayanti, and Sita, and a thoughtful Providence so arranged things that he grew to the exact stature that his manager required, and then growth ceased.

Since everyone saw how small Nilkanta was, and he himself felt small, he did not receive due respect for his years. Due to causes, natural and artificial, combined to make him sometimes seem immature for seventeen years, and at other times a mere lad of fourteen but far too knowing even for seventeen. And as no sign of hair appeared on his face, the confusion became greater. Either because he smoked or because he used language beyond his years, his lips puckered into lines that showed him to be old and hard, but innocence and youth shone in his large eyes.

In the quiet shelter of Sharat's house and garden at Chandernagore, nature had leisure to work her way unimpeded. Nilkanta had lingered in a kind of unnatural youth, but now he silently and swiftly overpassed that stage. His seventeen or eighteen years came to adequate revelation. No one observed the change, and its first sign was this, that when Kiran treated him like a boy, he felt ashamed. When the gay Kiran one day proposed that he should play the part of lady's companion, the idea of woman's dress hurt him, though he could not say why. So now, when she called for him to act over again his old characters, he disappeared.

It never occurred to Nilkanta that he was even now not much more than a lad-of-all-work in a strolling company. He even made up his mind to pick up a little education from Sharat's factor. But, because he was the pet of his master's wife, the factor could not endure the sight of him. Also, his restless training made it impossible for him to keep his mind long engaged, sooner or later, the alphabet did a misty dance before his eyes.

He would sit long enough with an open book on his lap, leaning against a *champak* bush beside the Ganges. The waves sighed below, boats floated past, birds flitted and twittered restlessly above. What thoughts passed through his mind as he looked down on that book he alone knew, if indeed he did know. He never advanced from one word to another, but the glorious thought, that he was actually reading a book, filled his soul with exultation. Whenever a boat went by, he lifted his book, and pretended to be reading hard, shouting at the top of his voice. But his energy dropped as soon as the audience was gone.

Formerly, he sang his songs automatically, but now their tunes stirred in his mind. Their words were of little import and full of trifling alliteration. Even the feeble meaning they had was beyond his comprehension, yet when he sang,

Twice-born bird, ah! wherefore stirred
To wrong our royal lady?
Goose, ah, say why wilt thou slay
Her in forest shady?

Then he felt as if transported to another world and to fear other folk. This familiar earth and his own poor life became music, and he was transformed. That tale of the goose and the king's daughter flung upon the mirror of his mind, a picture of surpassing beauty. It is impossible to say what he imagined himself to be, but the destitute little slave of the theatrical troupe faded from his memory.

When with evening the child of want lies down, dirty and hungry, in his squalid home, and hears of prince and princess and fabled gold, then in the dark hovel with its dim flickering candle, his mind springs free from its bonds of poverty and misery and walks in fresh beauty and glowing raiment, strong beyond all fear of hindrance, through that fairy realm where everything is possible.

Even so, this drudge of wandering players fashioned himself and his world anew, as he moved in spirit amid his songs. The lapping water, rustling leaves, and calling birds, the Goddess who had given shelter to him, the helpless, the God-forsaken, her gracious, lovely face, her exquisite arms with their shining bangles, her rosy feet as soft as flower-petals, all these by some magic became one with the music of his song. When the singing ended, the mirage faded, and the Nilkanta of the stage appeared again, with his wild elf-locks. Fresh from the complaints of his neighbour, the owner of the despoiled mango-orchard, Sharat would come and box his ears and cuff him. The boy Nilkanta, the misleader of adoring youths, went forth once more, to make ever new mischief by land and water and in the branches that are above the earth.

Shortly after the advent of Nilkanta, Sharat's younger brother, Satish, came to spend his college vacation with them. Kiran was hugely pleased at finding a fresh occupation. She and Satish were of the same age, and the time passed pleasantly in games and quarrels and reconciliations and laughter and even tears. Suddenly she would clasp him over the eyes from behind with vermilion-stained hands, or she would write 'Monkey' on his back, or else she would bolt the door on him from the outside amidst peals of laughter. Satish in his turn did not take things lying down, he would steal her keys and rings, he would put pepper among her betel, and he would tie her to the bed when she was not looking.

Meanwhile, heaven only knows what possessed poor Nilkanta. He was suddenly filled with a bitterness which he must avenge on somebody or something. He thrashed his devoted boy-followers for no fault, and sent them away crying. He would kick his pet mongrel till it made the skies resound with its whinings. When he went out for a walk, he would litter his path with twigs and leaves beaten from the roadside shrubs with his cane.

Kiran liked to see people enjoying good fare. Nilkanta had an immense capacity for eating, and never refused a good thing however often it was offered. So, Kiran liked to send for him to have his meals in her presence, and ply him with delicacies, happy in the bliss of seeing this Brahmin boy eat to satiety. After Satish's arrival she had much less spare time on her hands, and was seldom present when Nilkanta's meals were served. Before, her absence made no difference to the boy's appetite, and he would not rise till he had drained his cup of milk and rinsed it thoroughly with water.

But now, if Kiran was not present to ask him to try this and that, he was miserable, and nothing tasted right. He would get up, without eating much, and say to the serving-maid in a choking voice, "I am not hungry." In his imagination, the news of his repeated refusal, "I am not hungry," would reach Kiran, he pictured her concern, and hoped that she would send for him, and press him to eat. But nothing of the sort happened. Kiran never knew and never sent for him, and the maid finished whatever he left. He would then put out the lamp in his room, and throw himself on his bed in the darkness, burying his head in the pillow in a paroxysm of sobs. What was his grievance? Against whom? And from whom did he expect redress? At last, when no one else came, Mother Sleep soothed with her soft caresses the wounded heart of the motherless lad.

Nilkanta came to the unshakable conviction that Satish was poisoning Kiran's mind against him. If Kiran was absent-minded, and had not her usual smile, he would jump to the conclusion that some trick of Satish had made her angry with him. He took to praying to the Gods, with all the fervour of his hate, to make him at the next rebirth Satish, and Satish him.

He had an idea that a Brahmin's wrath could never be in vain, and the more he tried to consume Satish with the fire of his curses, the more did his own heart burn within him. And upstairs he would hear Satish laughing and joking with his sister-in-law.

Nilkanta never dared openly to show his enmity to Satish. But he would contrive a hundred petty ways of causing him annoyance. When Satish went for a swim in the river, and left his soap on the steps of the bathing-place, on coming back for it he would find that it had disappeared. Once he found his favourite striped tunic floating past him on the water, and thought it had been blown away by the wind.

One day Kiran, desiring to entertain Satish, sent for Nilkanta to recite as usual, but he stood there in gloomy silence. Quite surprised, Kiran asked him what was the matter. But he remained silent. And when again pressed by her to repeat some particular favourite piece of hers, he answered, "I don't remember" and walked away.

At last, the time came to return home. Everybody was busy packing up. Satish was going with them. But to Nilkanta, nobody said a word. The question whether he was to go or not seemed to have occurred to nobody.

The subject, as a matter of fact, had been raised by Kiran, who had proposed to take him along with them. But her husband and his mother and brother had all objected so strenuously that she let the matter drop. A couple of days before they were to start, she sent for the boy, and with kind words advised him to go back to his own home.

So many days had he felt neglected that this touch of kindness was too much for him, and he burst into tears. Kiran's eyes were also brimming over. She was filled with remorse at the thought that she had created a tie of affection, which could not be permanent.

But Satish was much annoyed at the blubbering of this overgrown boy. "Why does the fool stand there howling instead of speaking?" said he. When Kiran scolded him for an unfeeling creature, he replied, "My dear sister, you do not understand. You are too good and trustful. This fellow turns up from the Lord knows where, and is treated like a king. Naturally the tiger has no wish to become a mouse again. And he has evidently discovered that there is nothing like a tear or two to soften your heart."

Nilkanta hurriedly left the spot. He felt he would like to be a knife to cut Satish to pieces, a needle to pierce him through and through, and a fire to burn him to ashes. But Satish was not even scared. It was only his heart that bled and bled.

Satish had brought with him from Calcutta a grand inkstand. The inkpot was set in a mother-of-pearl boat drawn by a German-silver goose supporting a penholder. It was a great favourite of his, and he cleaned it carefully every day with an old silk handkerchief. Kiran would laugh, and tapping the silver bird's beak would say,

> *Twice-born bird, ah! wherefore stirred*
> *To wrong our royal lady?*

And the usual war of words would break out between her and her brother-in-law.

The day before they were to start, the inkstand was missing and could nowhere be found. Kiran smiled and said, "Brother-in-law, your goose has flown off to look for your Damayanti."

But Satish was in a great rage. He was certain that Nilkanta had stolen it as several people had said that they had seen him prowling about the room the night before. He had the accused brought before him. Kiran was also present. "You have stolen my inkstand, you thief!" he blurted out, "Bring it back at once." Nilkanta had always taken punishment from Sharat, deserved or undeserved, with perfect equanimity. But, when he was called a thief in Kiran's presence, his eyes blazed with a fierce anger, his breast swelled, and his throat choked. If Satish had said another word, he would have flown at him like a wild cat and used his nails like claws.

Kiran was greatly distressed at the scene, and taking the boy into another room said in her sweet, kind way, "Nilu, if you really have taken that inkstand give it to me quietly, and I shall see that no one says another word to you about it." Big tears coursed down the boy's cheeks, till at last he hid his face in his hands, and wept bitterly. Kiran came back from the room and said, "I am sure Nilkanta has not taken the inkstand." Sharat and Satish were equally positive that no other than Nilkanta could have done it.

But Kiran said determinedly, "Never!"

Sharat wanted to cross-examine the boy, but his wife refused to allow it.

Then Satish suggested that his room and box should be searched. And Kiran said, "If you dare do such a thing I will never forgive you. You shall not spy on the poor innocent boy." And as she spoke, her wonderful eyes filled with tears. That settled the matter and effectually prevented any further molestation of Nilkanta.

Kiran's heart overflowed with pity at this attempted outrage on a homeless lad. She got two new suits of clothes and a pair of shoes, and with these and a banknote in her hand she quietly went into Nilkanta's room in the evening. She intended to put these parting presents into his box as a surprise. The box itself had been her gift.

From her bunch of keys she selected one that fitted and noiselessly opened the box. It was so jumbled up with odds and ends that the new clothes would not go in. So she thought she had better take everything out and pack the box for him. At first knives, tops, kite-flying reels, bamboo twigs, polished shells for peeling green mangoes, bottoms of broken tumblers and such like things dear to a boy's heart were discovered. Then there came a layer of linen, clean and otherwise. And from under the linen there emerged the missing inkstand, goose and all.

Kiran, with flushed face, sat down helplessly with the inkstand in her hand, puzzled and wondering.

In the meantime, Nilkanta had come into the room from behind without Kiran knowing it. He had seen the whole thing and thought that Kiran had come like a thief to catch him in his thieving, and that his deed was out. How could he ever hope to convince her that he was not a thief, and that only revenge had prompted him to take the inkstand, which he meant to throw into the river at the first chance? In a weak moment he had put it in the box instead. "He was not a thief," his heart cried out, "Not a thief!" Then what was he? What could he say? That he had stolen, and yet he was not a thief? He could never explain to Kiran how grievously wrong she was. And then, how could he bear the thought that she had tried to spy on him?

At last Kiran with a deep sigh replaced the inkstand in the box, and, as if she were the thief herself, covered it up with the linen and the trinkets as they were before, and at the top she placed the presents, together with the banknote which she had brought for him.

The next day the boy was nowhere to be found. The villagers had not seen him, the police could discover no trace of him. Sharat said, "Now, as a matter of curiosity, let us have a look at his box." But Kiran was obstinate in her refusal to allow that to be done.

She had the box brought up to her own room, and taking out the inkstand alone, she threw it into the river.

The whole family went home. In a day the garden became desolate. And only that starving mongrel of Nilkanta's remained prowling along the river-bank, whining and whining as if its heart would break.

9
The Skeleton

In the room next to the one in which we used to sleep, there hung a human skeleton. In the night it would rattle in the breeze which played about its bones. In the day these bones were rattled by us. We were taking lessons in osteology from a student in the Campbell Medical School, for our guardians were determined to make us master of all sciences. How far they succeeded we need not tell those who know us, and it is better hidden from those who do not.

Many years have passed since then. In the meantime, the skeleton has vanished from the room, and the science of osteology from our brains, leaving no trace behind.

The other day, our house was crowded with guests, and I had to pass the night in the same old room. In these now unfamiliar surroundings, sleep refused to come, and, as I tossed from side to side, I heard all the hours of the night chimed, one after another, by the church clock nearby. At length the lamp in the corner of the room, after some minutes of choking and spluttering, went out altogether. One or two bereavements had recently happened in the family, so the going out of the lamp naturally led me to thoughts of death. In the great arena of nature, I thought, the light of a lamp losing itself in eternal darkness, and the going out of the light of our little human lives, by day or by night, were much the same thing.

My train of thought recalled my mind to the skeleton. While I was trying to imagine what the body which had clothed it could have been like, it suddenly seemed to me that something was walking round and round my bed, groping along the walls of the room. I could hear its rapid breathing. It seemed as if it was searching for something which it could not find, and pacing round the room with ever hastier steps. I felt quite sure that this was a mere fancy of my sleepless, excited brain, and that the throbbing of the veins in my temples was really the sound which seemed like running footsteps. Nevertheless, a cold shiver ran all over me. To help to get rid of this hallucination, I called out aloud, "Who is there?" The footsteps seemed to stop at my bedside, and the reply came, "It is me. I have come to look for that skeleton of mine."

It seemed absurd to show any fear before the creature of my own imagination, so, clutching my pillow a little more tightly, I said in a casual sort of way, "A nice business for this time of night! Of what use will that skeleton be to you now?"

The reply seemed to come almost from my mosquito-curtain itself, "What a question! In that skeleton were the bones that encircled my heart, the youthful charm of my six-and-twenty years bloomed about it. Should I not desire to see it once more?"

"Of course," said I, "a perfectly reasonable desire. Well, go on with your search, while I try to get a little sleep."

Said the voice, "But I fancy you are lonely. All right, I'll sit down a while, and we will have a little chat. Years ago I used to sit by men and talk to them. But during the last thirty-five years I have only moaned in the wind in the burning-places of the dead. I would talk once more with a man just like old times."

I felt that someone sat down just near my curtain. Resigning myself to the situation, I replied with as much cordiality as I could summon, "That will be very nice indeed. Let us talk of something cheerful."

"The funniest thing I can think of is my own life-story. Let me tell you that," said the voice.

The church clock chimed the hour of two.

"When I was in the land of the living and young, I feared one thing like death itself, and that was my husband. My feelings can be likened only to those of a fish caught with a hook. For it was as if a stranger had snatched me away with the sharpest of hooks from the peaceful calm of my childhood's home and from him I had no means of escape. My husband died two months after my marriage, and my friends and relations moaned pathetically on my behalf. My husband's father, after scrutinising my face with great care, said to my mother-in-law, 'Do you not see, she has the evil eye?'"

She stopped and asked, "Well, are you listening?"

"Very much indeed!" said I, "The beginning is extremely humorous."

"Let me proceed then. I came back to my father's house in great glee. People tried to conceal it from me, but I knew well that I was endowed with a rare and radiant beauty. What is your opinion?"

"Very likely," I murmured. "But you must remember that I never saw you."

"What! Not seen me? What about that skeleton of mine? *Ha! Ha! Ha!* Never mind. I was only joking. How can I ever make you believe that those two cavernous hollows contained the brightest of dark, languishing eyes? And that the smile which was revealed by those ruby lips had no resemblance whatever to the grinning teeth which you used to see? The mere attempt to convey to you some idea of the grace, the charm, the soft, firm, dimpled curves, which in the fullness of youth were growing and blossoming over those dry old bones makes me smile, it also makes me angry. The most eminent doctors of my time could not have dreamed of the bones of that body of mine as materials for teaching osteology. Do you know, one young doctor that I knew of, actually compared me to a golden *champak* blossom.

It meant that to him the rest of humankind was fit only to illustrate the science of physiology, that I was a flower of beauty. Does anyone think of the skeleton as beautiful as the *champak* flower?

"When I walked, I felt like a diamond scattering splendour, my every movement set waves of beauty radiating on every side. I used to spend hours gazing at my hands, which could have gracefully reined the liveliest of male creatures.

"But that stark and staring old skeleton of mine has borne false-witness to you against me, while I was unable to refute the shameless libel. That is why of all men I hate you the most! I feel I would like once and for all to banish sleep from your eyes with a vision of that warm rosy loveliness of mine, to sweep out with it all the wretched osteological stuff of which your brain is full."

"I could have sworn by your body," cried I, "if you had it still, that no vestige of osteology has remained in my head, and that the only thing that it is now full of is a radiant vision of perfect loveliness, glowing against the black background of night. I cannot say more than that."

"I had no girl-companions," went on the voice. "My only brother had made up his mind not to marry. In the zenana, I was alone. Alone I used to sit in the garden under the shade of the trees, and dream that the whole world was in love with me, that the stars with sleepless gaze were drinking in my beauty, that the wind was languishing in sighs as on some pretext or other it brushed past me, and that the lawn on which my feet rested, had it been conscious, would have lost consciousness again at their touch. It seemed to me that all the young men in the world were as blades of grass at my feet, and my heart, I know not why, used to grow sad."

"When my brother's friend, Shekhar, had passed out of the Medical College, he became our family doctor. I had already often seen him from behind a curtain. My brother was a strange man, and did not care to look on the world with open eyes. It was not empty enough for his taste, so he gradually moved away from it, until he was quite lost in an obscure corner. Shekhar was his only friend, so he was the only young man I could ever get to see. And when I held my evening court in my garden, then the host of imaginary young men whom I had at my feet were each one a Shekhar."

"Are you listening? What are you thinking of?" asked the voice.

I sighed as I replied, "I wish I was Shekhar!"

"Wait a bit. Hear the whole story first. One day, in the rains, I was feverish. The doctor came to see me. That was our first meeting. I was reclining opposite the window, so that the blush of the evening sky might temper the pallor of my complexion. When the doctor came in, he looked up into my face. I put myself into his place, and gazed at myself in imagination. I saw in the glorious evening light that delicate wan face laid like a drooping flower against the soft white pillow, with the unrestrained curls playing over the forehead, and the bashfully lowered eyelids casting a pathetic shade over the whole countenance."

The doctor, in a tone bashfully low, asked my brother, "May I feel her pulse?"

"I put out a tired, well-rounded wrist from beneath the coverlet. Ah! thought I, as I looked on it, 'if only there had been a sapphire bracelet.' I have never before seen a doctor so awkward about feeling a patient's pulse. His fingers trembled as they felt my wrist. He measured the heat of my fever, I gauged the pulse of his heart. Don't you believe me?"

"Very easily," said I, "the human heart-beat tells its tale."

"After I had been taken ill and restored to health several times, I found that the number of the courtiers who attended my imaginary evening reception began to dwindle till they were reduced to only one! And at last in my little world there remained only one doctor and one patient.

"In these evenings I used to dress myself secretly in a canary-coloured sari, twine about the braided knot into which I did my hair a garland of white jasmine blossoms, and with a little mirror in my hand betake myself to my usual seat under the trees.

"Well! Are you perhaps thinking that the sight of one's own beauty would soon grow wearisome? Ah no! for I did not see myself with my own eyes. I was then one and also two. I used to see myself as though I were the doctor, I gazed, I was charmed, I fell madly in love. But, in spite of all the caresses I lavished on myself, a sigh would wander about my heart, moaning like the evening breeze.

"Anyhow, from that time I was never alone. When I walked I watched with downcast eyes the play of my dainty little toes on the earth, and wondered what the doctor would have felt had he been there to see. At mid-day the sky would be filled with the glare of the sun, without a sound, save now and then the distant cry of a passing kite. Outside our garden-walls the hawker would pass with his musical cry of "Bangles for sale, crystal bangles." And I, spreading a snow-white sheet on the lawn, would lie on it with my head on my arm. With studied carelessness the other arm would rest lightly on the soft sheet, and I would imagine to myself that someone had caught sight of the wonderful pose of my hand, that someone had clasped it in both of his and imprinted a kiss on its rosy palm, and was slowly walking away. What if I ended the story here? How would it do?"

"Not half a bad ending," I replied thoughtfully, "It would no doubt remain a little incomplete, but I could easily spend the rest of the night putting in the finishing touches."

"But that would make the story too serious. Where would the laugh come in? Where would be the skeleton with its grinning teeth?

"So let me go on. As soon as the doctor had got a little practice, he took a room on the ground-floor of our house for a consulting-chamber. I used then sometimes to ask him jokingly about medicines and poisons, and how much of this drug or that would kill a man. The subject was congenial and he would wax eloquent. These talks familiarised me with the idea of death, and so love and death were the only two things that filled my little world. My story is now nearly ended and there is not much left."

"Not much of the night is left either," I muttered.

"After a time I noticed that the doctor had grown strangely absent-minded, and it seemed as if he were ashamed of something which he was trying to keep from me. One day he came in, somewhat smartly dressed and borrowed my brother's carriage for the evening.

"My curiosity became too much for me, and I went up to my brother for information. After some talk beside the point, I at last asked him, "By the way, Dada, where is the doctor going this evening in your carriage?"

"My brother briefly replied, "To his death."

"Oh, do tell me," I importuned, "Where is he really going?"

"To be married," he said, a little more explicitly.

"Oh, indeed!" said I, as I laughed long and loudly.

"I gradually learnt that the bride was an heiress, who would bring the doctor a large sum of money. But why did he insult me by hiding all this from me? Had I ever begged and prayed him not to marry, because it would break my heart? Men are not to be trusted. I have known only one man in all my life, and in a moment I made this discovery.

"When the doctor came in after his work and was ready to start, I said to him, rippling with laughter the while, "Well, doctor, so you are to be married tonight?"

"My gaiety not only made the doctor lose countenance, it thoroughly irritated him."

"How is it," I went on, "that there is no illumination, no band of music?"

With a sigh he replied, "Is marriage then such a joyful occasion?"

I burst out into renewed laughter. "No, no," said I, "this will never do. Who ever heard of a wedding without lights and music?"

I bothered my brother about it so much that he at once ordered all the trappings of a gay wedding. All the time I kept on gaily talking of the bride, of what would happen, of what I would do when the bride came home.

"Doctor," I asked, "will you still go on feeling pulses?" *Ha! Ha! Ha!* Though the inner workings of people's, especially men's, minds are not visible, still I can take my oath that these words were piercing the doctor's bosom like deadly darts.

"The marriage was to be celebrated late at night. Before starting, the doctor and my brother were having a glass of wine together on the terrace, as was their daily habit. The moon had just risen.

"I went up smiling, and said, "Have you forgotten your wedding, doctor? It is time to start."

"I must here tell you one little thing. I had meanwhile gone down to the dispensary and got a little powder, which at a convenient opportunity I had dropped unobserved into the doctor's glass.

"The doctor, draining his glass at a gulp, in a voice thick with emotion, and with a look that pierced me to the heart, said, "Then I must take my leave."

"The music struck up. I went into my room and dressed myself in my bridal-robes of silk and gold. I took out my jewellery and ornaments from the safe and put them all on, I put the red mark of wifehood on the parting in my hair. And then under the tree in the garden I prepared my bed.

"It was a beautiful night. The gentle south wind was kissing away the weariness of the world. The scent of jasmine and bela filled the garden with rejoicing.

"When the sound of the music began to grow fainter and fainter, the light of the moon to get dimmer and dimmer, the world with its lifelong associations of home and kin to fade away from my perceptions like some illusion, then I closed my eyes, and smiled.

"I fancied that when people came and found me they would see that smile of mine lingering on my lips like a trace of rose-coloured wine, that when I thus slowly entered my eternal bridal-chamber I should carry with me this smile, illuminating my face. But alas for the bridal-chamber! Alas for the bridal-robes of silk and gold! When I woke at the sound of a rattling within me, I found three urchins learning osteology from my skeleton. Where in my bosom my joys and griefs used to throb, and the petals of youth to open one by one, there the master with his pointer was busy naming my bones. "Well, well, how did you like the story?" asked the voice.

"It has been delightful," said I.

At this point, the first crow began to caw.

"Are you there?" I asked. There was no reply.

The morning light entered the room.

10
The Auspicious Vision

Kantichandra was young, yet after his wife's death he sought no second partner and gave his mind to the hunting of beasts and birds. His body was long and slender, hard and agile, his sight keen, his aim unerring. He dressed like a countryman and took with him Hira Singh the wrestler, Chakkanlal, Khan Saheb the musician, Mian Saheb, and many others. He had no lack of idle followers.

In the month of Agrahayan, Kanti had gone out shooting near the swamp of Nydighi with a few sporting companions. They were in boats, and an army of servants, in boats also, filled the bathing-ghats. The village women found it well-nigh impossible to bathe or to draw water. All day long, land and water trembled to the firing of the guns, and every evening the musicians killed the only chance to sleep.

One morning as Kanti was seated in his boat cleaning a favourite gun, he suddenly started at what he thought was the cry of a wild duck. Looking up, he saw a village maiden, coming to the water's edge, with two white ducklings clasped to her breast. The little stream was almost stagnant. Many weeds choked the current. The girl put the birds into the water and watched them anxiously. Evidently, the presence of the sportsmen was the cause of her care and not the wildness of the ducks.

The girl's beauty had a rare freshness as if she had just come from Vishwakarma's workshop. It was difficult to guess her age. Her figure was almost a woman's, but her face was so childish that clearly, the world had left no impression there. She seemed not to know herself that she had reached the threshold of youth.

Kanti's stopped cleaning his gun for a while. He was fascinated. He had not expected to see such a face in such a spot. And yet its beauty suited its surroundings better than it would have suited a palace. A bud is lovelier on the bough than in a golden vase. That day the blossoming reeds glittered in the autumn dew and morning sun, and the fresh, simple face set in the midst was like a picture of the festival to Kanti's enchanted mind. Kalidas has forgotten to sing how Siva's Mountain-Queen herself sometimes has come to the young Ganges, with ducklings close to her breast. As he gazed, the maiden stared in terror, and hurriedly took back the ducks into her bosom, uttering a cry of pain. In another moment, she left the riverbank and disappeared into the bamboo thicket hard by. Looking around, Kanti saw one of his men pointing an unloaded gun at the ducks. He at once went up to him, wrenched away from his gun, and bestowed on his cheek a prodigious slap. The astonished humourist finished his joke on the floor. Kanti went on cleaning his gun.

But curiosity drove Kanti to the thicket wherein he had seen the girl disappear. Pushing his way through, he found himself in the yard of a well-to-do householder. On one side was a row of conical thatched barns, on the other a clean cow-shed, at the end of which grew a Jujube bush. Under the bush was seated the girl he had seen that morning, sobbing over a wounded dove, into whose yellow beak she was trying to bring a little water from the moist corner of her garment. A grey cat, its fore-paws on her knee, was looking eagerly at the bird, and every now and then, when it got too forward, she kept it in its place by a warning tap on the nose.

This little picture, set in the peaceful mid-day surroundings of the householder's yard, instantly impressed itself on Kanti's sensitive heart. The checkered light and shade, flickering beneath the delicate foliage of the Jujube, played on the girl's lap. Not far off, a cow was chewing the cud, and lazily keeping off the flies with slow movements of its head and tail. The north wind whispered softly in the rustling bamboo thickets. And she who at dawn on the river-bank had looked like the Mountain-Queen, now in the silence of noon showed the eager pity of the divine housewife. Kanti, coming in upon her with his gun, had a sense of intrusion. He felt like a thief caught red-handed. He longed to explain that it was not he who had hurt the dove. As he wondered how he should begin, there came a call of "Sudha!" from the house. The girl jumped up. "Sudha!" came the voice again. She took up her dove, and ran within. "Sudha," thought Kanti, "what an appropriate name!"

Kanti returned to the boat, handed his gun to his men, and went over to the front door of the house. He found a middle-aged Brahmin, with a peaceful, clean-shaven face, seated on a bench outside, and reading a devotional book. Kanti saw in his kindly, thoughtful face something of the tenderness which shone in the face of the maiden.

Kanti saluted him, and said, "May I ask for some water, sir? I am very thirsty." The elder man welcomed him with eager hospitality, and, offering him a seat on the bench, went inside and fetched with his own hands a little brass plate of sugar wafers and a bell-metal vessel full of water.

After Kanti had eaten and drunk, the Brahmin begged him to introduce himself. Kanti gave his own name, his father's name, and the address of his home, and then said in the usual way, "If I can be of any service, sir, I shall deem myself fortunate."

"I require no service, my son," said Nabin Banerji, "I have only one care at present."

"What is that, sir?" said Kanti.

"It is my daughter, Sudha, who is growing up, for whom I have not yet been able to find a worthy bridegroom. If I could only see her well married, all my debt to this world would be paid. But there is no suitable bridegroom here, and I cannot leave my charge of Gopinath here, to search for a husband elsewhere."

"If you would see me in my boat, sir, we would have a talk about the marriage of your daughter." So saying, Kanti repeated his salute and went back. He then sent some of his men into the village to inquire, and in answer heard nothing but praise of the beauty and virtues of the Brahmin's daughter.

When next day the old man came to the boat on his promised visit, Kanti bent low in salutation and begged the hand of his daughter for himself. The Brahmin was so much overcome by this undreamed-of piece of good fortune for Kanti not only belonged to a well-known Brahmin family but was also a landed proprietor of wealth and position that at first he could hardly utter a word in reply. He thought there must have been some mistake, and at length mechanically repeated, "You desire to marry my daughter?"

"If you will deign to give her to me," said Kanti.

"You mean Sudha?" he asked again.

"Yes," was the reply.

"But will you not first see and speak to her?"

Kanti, pretending he had not seen her already, said, "Oh that we shall do at the moment of the Auspicious Vision."

In a voice husky with emotion the old man said, "My Sudha is indeed a good girl, well skilled in all the household arts. As you are so generously taking her on trust, may she never cause you a moment's regret? This is my blessing!"

The brick-built mansion of the Mazumdars had been borrowed for the wedding ceremony, which was fixed for next Magh, as Kanti did not wish to delay. In due time the bridegroom arrived on his elephant, with drums and music and with a torchlight procession, and the ceremony began.

When the bridal couple was covered with the scarlet screen for the rite of the Auspicious Vision, Kanti looked up at his bride. In that bashful, downcast face, crowned with the wedding coronet and bedecked with sandal paste, he could scarcely recognise the village maiden of his fancy, and in the fullness of his emotion, a mist seemed to becloud his eyes.

At the gathering of women in the bridal chamber, after the wedding ceremony was over, an old village dame insisted that Kanti himself should take off his wife's bridal veil. As he did so he started back. It was not the same girl.

Something rose from within his breast and pierced into his brain. The light of the lamps seemed to grow dim, and darkness to tarnish the face of the bride herself.

At first, he felt angry with his father-in-law. The old scoundrel had shown him one girl and married him to another. But on calmer reflection, he remembered that the old man had not shown him any daughter at all that it was his own fault. He thought it best not to show his arrant folly to the world and took his place again with apparent calmness.

He could swallow the powder, he could not get rid of its taste. He could not bear the merry-makings of the festive throng. He was in a blaze of anger with himself as well as with everybody else.

Suddenly he felt the bride, seated by his side, who gave a little start and a suppressed scream by seeing a leveret scampering into the room, which had brushed across her feet. Close upon it followed the girl he had seen before. She caught up the leveret into her arms and began to caress it with an affectionate murmuring. "Oh, the mad girl!" cried the women as they made signs to her to leave the room. She heeded them not, however, but came and unconcernedly sat in front of the wedded pair, looking into their faces with childish curiosity. When a maidservant came and took her by the arm to lead her away, Kanti hurriedly interposed saying, "Let her be."

"What is your name?" he then went on to ask her.

The girl swayed backwards and forwards but gave no reply. All the women in the room began to titter.

Kanti put another question, "Have those ducklings of yours grown up?"

The girl stared at him as unconcernedly as before.

The bewildered Kanti screwed up courage for another effort, and asked tenderly after the wounded dove, but with no avail. The increasing laughter in the room betokened an amusing joke.

At last Kanti learned that the girl was deaf and dumb, the companion of all the animals and birds of the locality. It was but by chance that she rose the other day when the name of Sudha was called.

Kanti now received a second shock. A black screen lifted from before his eyes. With a sigh of intense relief, as of escape from calamity, he looked once more into the face of his bride. Then came the true Auspicious Vision. The light from his heart and from the smokeless lamps fell on her gracious face, and he saw it in its true radiance, knowing that Nabin's blessing would find fulfillment.

11
Living or Dead?

I

The widow in the house of Saradasankar, the Ranihat zamindar, had no kinsmen of her father's family. One after another all had died. Nor had she in her husband's family any one she could call her own, neither husband nor a son. The child of her brother-in-law Saradasankar was her darling. For a long time after his birth, his mother had been very ill, and the widow, his aunt Kadambini, had fostered him. If a woman fosters another's child, her love for him is all the stronger because she has no claim upon him no claim of kinship, that is, but simply the claim of love. Love cannot prove its claim by any document which society accepts, and does not wish to prove it, it merely worships with double passion its life's uncertain treasure. Thus the entire widow's thwarted love went out to wards this little child. One night in Shravan, Kadambini died suddenly. For some reason her heart stopped beating. Everywhere else the world held on its course, only in this gentle little breast, suffering with love, the watch of time stood still forever.

Lest they should be harassed by the poike, four of the zamindar's Brahmin servants took away the body, without any ceremony, to be burned. The burning-ground of Ranihat was very far from the village. There was a hut beside a tank, a huge banian near it, and nothing more. Formerly a river, now completely dried up, ran through the ground, and part of the watercourse had been dug out to make a tank for the performance of funeral rites. The people considered the tank as part of the river and reverenced it as such.

Taking the body into the hut, the four men sat down to wait for the wood. The time seemed so long that two of the four grew restless, and went to see why it did not come. Nitai and Gurucharan being gone, Bidhu and Banamali remained to watch over the body.

It was a dark night of Shravan. Heavy clouds hung in a starless sky. The two men sat silently in the dark room. Their matches and lamp were useless. The matches were damp, and would not light, for all their efforts, and the lantern went out.

After a long silence, one said, "Brother, it would be good if we had a bowl of tobacco. In our hurry we brought none."

The other answered, "I can run and bring all we want."

Understanding why Banarnali wanted to go (From fear of ghosts, the burning-ground being considered haunted), Bidhu said, "I daresay! Meanwhile, I suppose I am to sit here alone!"

Conversation ceased again. Five minutes seemed like an hour. In their minds they cursed the two, who had gone to fetch the wood, and they began to suspect that they sat gossiping in some pleasant nook. There was no sound anywhere, except the incessant noise of frogs and crickets from the tank. Then suddenly they fancied that the bed shook slightly, as if the dead body had turned on its side. Bidhu and Banamali trembled, and began muttering, "*Ram! Ram!*". A deep sigh was heard in the room. In a moment the watchers leapt out of the hut, and raced for the village.

After running about three miles, they met their colleagues coming back with a lantern. As a matter of fact, they had gone to smoke, and knew nothing about the wood. But they declared that a tree had been cut down, and that, when it was split up, it would be brought along at once. Then Bidhu and Banamali told them what had happened in the hut. Nitai and Gurucharan scoffed at the story, and abused Bidhu and Banamali angrily for leaving their duty.

Without delay all four returned to the hut. As they entered, they saw at once that the body was gone, nothing but an empty bed remained. They stared at one another. Could a jackal have taken it? But there was no scrap of clothing anywhere. Going outside, they saw that on the mud that had collected at the door of the hut there were a woman's tiny footprints, newly made. Saradasankar was no fool, and they could hardly persuade him to believe in this ghost story. So after much discussion the four decided that it would be best to say that the body had been burnt.

Towards dawn, when the men with the wood arrived they were told that, owing to their delay, the work had been done without them, there had been some wood in the hut after all. No one was likely to question this, since a dead body is not such a valuable property that anyone would steal it.

II

Everyone knows that, even when there is no sign, life is often secretly present, and may begin again in an apparently dead body. Kadambini was not dead, only the machine of her life had for some reason suddenly stopped.

When consciousness returned, she saw dense darkness on all sides. It occurred to her that she was not lying in her usual place. She called out, "Sister," but no answer came from the darkness. As she sat up, terror-stricken, she remembered her death-bed, the sudden pain at her breast, the beginning of a choking sensation. Her elder sister-in-law was warming some milk for the child, when Kadambini became faint, and fell on the bed, saying with a choking voice, "Sister, bring the child here. I am worried."

After that everything went black, as when an inkpot is upset over an exercise-book. Kadambini's memory and consciousness, all the letters of the world's book, in a moment became formless. The widow could not remember whether the child, in the sweet voice of love, called her, "Auntie," as if for the last time, or not, she could not remember whether, as she left the world she knew for death's endless unknown journey, she had received a parting gift of affection, love's passage-money for the silent land. At first, I fancy, she thought the lonely dark place was the House of Yama, where there is nothing to see, nothing to hear, nothing to do, only an eternal watch. But when a cold damp wind drove through the open door, and she heard the croaking of frogs, she remembered vividly and in a moment all the rains of her short life, and could feel her kinship with the earth. Then came a flash of lightning, and she saw the tank, the banian, the great plain, the far-off trees. She remembered how at full moon she had sometimes come to bathe in this tank, and how dreadful death had seemed when she saw a corpse on the burning-ground.

Her first thought was to return home. But then she reflected, "I am dead. How can I return home? That would bring disaster on them. I have left the kingdom of the living, I am my own ghost!" If this were not so, she reasoned, how could she have got out of Saradasankar's well-guarded zenana, and come to this distant burning ground at midnight? Also, if her funeral rites had not been finished, where had the men gone who should burn her? Recalling her death-moment in Saradasankar's brightly-lit house, she now found herself alone in a distant, deserted, dark burning ground. Surely she was no member of earthly society! Surely she was a creature of horror, of ill-omen, her own ghost!

At this thought, all the bonds were snapped which bound her to the world. She felt that she had marvellous strength and endless freedom. She could do what she liked, go where she pleased. Mad with the inspiration of this new idea, she rushed from the house but like a gust of wind, and stood upon the burning- ground. All trace of shame or fear had left her.

But as she walked on and on, her feet grew tired her body weak. The plain stretched on endlessly, here and there were paddy-fields, sometimes she found herself standing knee-deep in water.

At the first glimmer of dawn, she heard one or two birds cry from the bamboo-clumps of the distant houses. Then terror seized her. She could not tell in what new relation she stood to the earth and the living folk. As long as she been on the plain, on the burning-ground, covered by the dark night of Shravan, she had been fearless- a denizen of her own kingdom. By daylight the homes of men filled her with fear. Men and ghosts dread each other, for their tribes inhabit different banks of the river of death.

III

Her clothes were clotted in the mud, strange thoughts and walking by night had given her the aspect of a madwoman, truly, her apparition was such that folk might have been afraid of her, and children might have stoned her or ran away. Luckily, the first to catch sight of her was a traveller. He came up, and said, "Mother, you look, like a respectable woman. Wherever are you going, alone and in this guise?"

Kadambini, unable to collect her thoughts, stared at him in silence. She could not think that she was still in touch with the world, that she looked like a respectable woman, that a traveller was asking her questions.

Again the man said, "Come, mother, I will see you home. Tell me where you live."

Kadambini thought that returning to her father-in-law's house would be absurd, and she had no father's house.

Then she remembered the friend from her childhood. She had not seen Jogmaya since the days of her youth, but from time to time they had exchanged letters. Occasionally there had been quarrels between them, as was only right, since Kadambini wished to make it clear that her love for Jogmaya was unbounded, while her friend complained that Kadambini did not return a love equal to her own. They were both sure that, if they once met, they would be inseparable.

Kadambini said to the traveller, "I will go to Sripati's house at Nisindapur."

As he was going to Calcutta, Nisindapur, though not near, was on his way. So he took Kadambini to Sripati's house, and the friends met again. At first they did not recognise one another, but gradually each recognised the features of the other's childhood.

"What luck!" said Jogmaya, "I never dreamt that I would see you again. But how have you come here, sister? Your father-in-law's folk surely didn't let you go!"

Kadambini remained silent, and at last said, "Sister, do not ask about my father-in-law. Give me a corner, and treat me as a servant, I will do your work."

"What?" cried Jogmaya. "Keep you like a servant! Why, you are my closest friend, you are my..." and their conversations continued.

Just then Sripati came in. Kadambini stared at him for some time, and then went out very slowly. She kept her head uncovered, and showed not the slightest modesty or respect. Jogmaya, fearing that Sripati would be prejudiced against her friend, began an elaborate explanation. But Sripati, who readily agreed to anything Jogmaya said, cut short her story, and left his wife uneasy in her mind.

Kadambini had come, but she was not at one with her friend, death was between them. She could feel no intimacy for others so long as her existence perplexed her and consciousness remained. Kadambini would look at Jogmaya, and brood. She would think, "She has her husband and her work, she lives in a world far away from mine. She shares affection and duty with the people of the world, I am an empty shadow. She is among the living, I am in eternity."

Jogmaya also was uneasy, but could not explain why. Women do not love mystery, because, though uncertainty may be transmuted into poetry, into heroism, into scholarship, it cannot be turned to account in household work. So, when a woman cannot understand a thing, she either destroys or forgets it, or she shapes it anew for her own use, if she fails to deal with it in one of these ways, she loses her temper with it. The greater Kadambini's abstraction became, the more impatient was Jogmaya with her, wondering what trouble weighed upon her mind.

Then a new danger arose. Kadambini was afraid of herself, yet she could not flee from herself. Those who fear ghosts fear those who are behind them, wherever they cannot see there is fear. But Kadambini's chief terror lay in herself, for she dreaded nothing external. At the dead of night, when alone in her room, she screamed, in the evening, when she saw her shadow in the lamp-light, her whole body shook. Watching her fearfulness, the rest of the house fell into a sort of terror. The servants and Jogmaya herself began to see ghosts.

One midnight, Kadambini came out from her bedroom weeping, and wailed at Jogmaya's door, "Sister, sister, let me lie at your feet! Do not put me by myself!"

Jogmaya's anger was no less than her fear. She would have liked to drive Kadambini from the house that very second. The good-natured Sripati, after much effort, succeeded in quieting their guest, and put her in the next room.

Next day, Sripati was unexpectedly summoned to his wife's apartment. She began to upbraid him, "You, do you call yourself, a man? A woman runs away from her father-in-law, and enters your house, a month passes, and you haven't hinted that she should go away, nor have I heard the slightest protest from you. I should take it as a favour if you would explain yourself. You men are all alike."

Men, as a race, have a natural partiality for womankind in general, foe which women themselves hold them accountable. Although Sripati was prepared to touch Jogmaya's body, and swear that his kind feeling towards the helpless but beautiful Kadambini was no whit greater than it should be, he could not prove it by his behaviour. He thought that her father-in-law's people must have treated this forlorn widow abominably, if she could bear it no longer, and was driven to take refuge with him. As she had neither father nor mother, how could he desert her? So saying, he let the matter drop, far he had no mind to distress Kadambini by asking her unpleasant questions.

His wife, then, tried other means of her sluggish lord, until at last he saw that for the sake of peace he must send word to Kadambini's father-in-law. The result of a letter, he thought, might not be satisfactory, so he resolved to go to Ranihat, and act on what he learnt.

So Sripati went, and Jogmaya on her part said to Kadambini, "Friend, it hardly seems proper for you to stop here any longer. What will people say?"

Kadambini stared solemnly at Jogmaya, and said, "What have I to do with people?"

Jogmaya was astounded. She said sharply, "If you have nothing to do with people, we have. How can we explain the detention of a woman belonging to another house?"

Kadambini said, "Where is my father-in-law's house?"

"Confound it!" thought Jogmaya, "What will the wretched woman say next?"

Very slowly Kadambini said, "What have I to do with you? Am I of the earth? You laugh, weep, love, each grips and holds his own, I merely look. You are human, I am just a shadow. I cannot understand why God has kept me in this world of yours."

So strange was her look that Jogmaya understood something of her drift, though not all. Unable to decide whether to dismiss her or to ask her, she went away, oppressed with thought.

IV

It was nearly ten o' clock at night when Sripati returned from Ranihat. The earth was drowned in torrents of rain. It seemed that the downpour would never stop, that the night would never end.

Jogmaya asked, "Well?"

"I've lots to say, presently," replied Sripati.

So saying, Sripati changed his clothes, and sat down to supper, and then he lay dawn for a smoke. His mind was perplexed.

His wife stilled her curiosity for a long time, came to his couch and demanded, "What did you hear?"

"That you have certainly made a mistake," said Sripati.

Jogmaya was nettled. Women never make mistakes, or, if they do, a sensible man never mentions them, it is better to take them on his own shoulders. Jogmaya snapped, "May I be permitted to hear how?"

Sripati replied, "The woman you have taken into your house is not your Kadambini." Hearing this, she was greatly annoyed, especially since it was her husband who said it. "What! I don't know my own friend? I must come to you to recognise her! You are clever, indeed!"

Sripati explained that there was no need to quarrel about his cleverness. He could prove what he said. There was no doubt that Jogmaya's Kadambini was dead.

Jogmaya replied, "Listen! You've certainly made some huge mistake. You've been to the wrong house, or are confused as to what you have heard. Who told you to go yourself? Write a letter, and everything will be cleared up."

Sripati was hurt by his wife's lack of faith and produced all sorts of proof, but in vain. Midnight found them still asserting and contradicting. Although they were both agreed now that Kadambini should be got out of the house, although Sripati believed that their guest had deceived his wife all the time by a pretended acquaintance, and Jogmaya that she was a prostitute, yet in the present discussion neither would acknowledge defeat. By degrees their voices got louder and they forgot that Kadambini was sleeping in the next room.

They kept on arguing. The one said, "We're in a nice fix! I tell you, I heard it with my own ears!" And the other answered angrily, "What do I care about that? I can see with my own eyes, surely."

At length Jogmaya said, "Very well. Tell me when Kadambini died." She thought that if she could find a discrepancy between the day of death and the date of some letter from Kadambini, she could prove that Sripati erred.

He told her the date of Kadambini's death, and both realized that it fell on the very day before she came to their house. Jogmaya's heart trembled, even Sripati was not unmoved.

Just then the door flew open, a damp wind swept in and blew the lamp out. The darkness rushed after it, and filled the whole house. Kadambini stood in the room. It was nearly one o' clock, the rain was pelting outside.

Kadambini spoke, "Friend, I am your Kadambini, but I am no longer living. I am dead."

Jogmaya screamed in terror, Sripati could not speak.

"But, save in being dead, I have done you no wrong. If I have no place among the living, I have none among the dead. Oh! Where shall I go?"

Crying as if to wake the sleeping Creator in the dense night of rain, she asked again, "Oh! Where shall I go?"

So, saying this, Kadambini left her friend fainting in the dark house and went out into the world, seeking her own place.

V

It is hard to say how Kadambini reached Ranihat. At first she showed herself to no one, but spent the whole day in a ruined temple, starving. During untimely afternoon of the rains when people huddled into their houses for fear of the impending storm, Kadambini came forth. Her heart trembled as she reached her father-in-law's house, and when, drawing a thick veil over her face, she entered, none of the doorkeepers objected, since they took her for a servant. And the rain was pouring down, and the wind howled.

The mistress, Saradasankar's wife, was playing cards with her widowed sister. A servant was in the kitchen, the sick child was sleeping in the bedroom. Kadambini, escaping every one's notice, entered this room. I do not know why she had come to her father-in-law's house, she herself did not know, she only felt the need to see her child again. She did not know where to go next, or what to do.

In the lighted room she saw the child sleeping, his fists clenched, his body wasted with fever. At the sight of him, her heart became parched and thirsty. If only she could press that tortured body to her breast! Immediately the thought followed, "I do not exist. Who would see it? His mother loves company, loves gossip and cards. All the time that she left me in charge, neither she was in anxiety, nor was she troubled about him in the least. Who will look after him now as I did?"

The child turned on his side, and cried, half-asleep, "Auntie, give me water." Her darling had not yet forgotten his auntie! In a fever of excitement, she poured out some water, and, taking him to her breast, she gave it him.

As long as he was asleep, the child felt no strangeness in taking water from the accustomed hand. But when Kadambini satisfied her long-starved longing, and kissed him and began rocking him asleep again, he awoke and embraced her.

"Did you die, Auntie?" he asked.

"Yes, darling," sobbed Kadambini.

"And you have come back? Do not die again," replied the child.

Before she could answer disaster overtook her. One of the maidservants coming in with a cup of sago dropped it, and fell down. At the crash the mistress left her cards, and entered the room. She stood like a pillar of wood, unable to flee or speak. Seeing all this, the child, too, became terrified, and burst out weeping, "Go away, Auntie," he said, "Go away!"

Now at last Kadambini understood that she had not died. The old room, the old things, the same child, the same love, all returned to their living state, without change or difference between her and them. In her friend's house she had felt that her childhood's companion was dead. In her child's room she knew that the boy's "Auntie" was not dead at all. In anguished tones she said, "Sister, why do you dread me? See, I am as you knew me."

Her sister-in-law could endure no longer, and fell into a faint. Saradasankar himself entered the zenana. With folded hands, he said piteously, "Is this right? Satish is my only son. Why do you show yourself to him? Are we not your own kin? Since you went, he has wasted away daily, his fever has been incessant, day and night he cries, "Auntie, Auntie." You have left the world, break these bonds of maya. We will perform all funeral honours."

Kadambini could bear no more. She said, "Oh, I am not dead, I am not dead. Oh, how can I persuade you that I am not dead? I am living, living!" She lifted a brass pot from the ground and dashed it against her forehead. The blood ran from her brow. "Look!" she cried, "I am living!" Saradasankar stood like an image, the child screamed with fear, the two fainting women lay still.

Then, Kadambini ran shouting, "I am not dead, I am not dead," and went down the steps to the zenana well and plunged in. From the upper storey Saradasankar heard the splash.

All night the rain poured, it poured next day at dawn, was pouring still at noon. Through death, Kadambini proved that she was not dead.

12
My Fair Neighbour

My feelings towards the young widow who lived in the next house to mine were of worship, at least, that is what I told to my friends and myself. Even my nearest intimate, Nabin, knew nothing of the real state of my mind. And I had a sort of pride that I could keep my passion pure by thus concealing it in the inmost recesses of my heart. She was like a dew-drenched sephali-blossom, untimely fallen to earth. Too radiant and holy for the flower-decked marriagebed, she had been dedicated to heaven.

But passion is like the mountain stream, and refuses to be enclosed in the place of its birth, and seeks an outlet. That is why I tried to give expression to my emotions in poems, but my unwilling pen refused to desecrate the object of my worship.

It happened curiously that just at this time my friend Nabin was afflicted with a madness of verse. It came upon him like an earthquake. It was the poor fellow's first attack, and he was equally unprepared for rhyme and rhythm. Nevertheless he could not refrain, for he succumbed to the fascination, as a widower to his second wife.

So, Nabin sought help from me. The subject of his poems were all addressed to the beloved one. I slapped his back in jest, and asked him, "Well, old chap, who is she?"

Nabin laughed, as he replied, "That I have not yet discovered!"

I confess that I found considerable comfort in bringing help to my friend. Like a hen brooding on a duck's egg, I lavished all the warmth of my pent-up passion on Nabin's effusions.

So vigorously did I revise and improve his crude productions, that the larger part of each poem became my own.

Then, Nabin would scream in surprise, "That is exactly what I wanted to say, but could not. How on earth do you manage to get hold of all these fine sentiments?"

I would reply poetically, "They come from my imagination, for, as you know, truth is silent, and it is imagination only which waxes eloquent. Reality represses the flow of feeling like a rock, imagination cuts out a path for itself."

And the poor puzzled Nabin would say, "Yes, I see. Yes, of course," and then after some thought would murmur again, "Yes, yes, you are right!"

As I have already said, in my own love there was a feeling of reverential delicacy which prevented me from putting it into words. But with Nabin as a screen, there was nothing to hinder the flow of my pen, and a true warmth of feeling gushed out into these vicarious poems.

Nabin in his lucid moments would say, "But these are yours! Let me publish them over your name."

"Nonsense!" I would reply, "They are yours, my dear fellow, I have only added a touch or two here and there." Nabin gradually came to believe it.

I will not deny that, with a feeling akin to that of the astronomer gazing into the starry heavens, I did sometimes turn my eyes towards the window of the house next door. It is also true that now and again my furtive glances would be rewarded with a vision. And the least glimpse of the pure light of that countenance would at once still and clarify all that was turbulent and unworthy in my emotions.

But one day, I was startled. It was a hot summer afternoon. One of the fierce and fitful norwesters was threatening. Black clouds massed in the north-west corner of the sky, and against the strange and fearful light of that background my fair neighbour stood, gazing out into empty space. And what a world of forlorn longing did I discover in the faraway look of those lustrous black eyes! Was there then, perchance, still some living volcano within the serene radiance of that moon of mine? Alas! that look of limitless yearning, which was winging its way through the clouds like an eager bird, surely sought the nest of some human heart!

At the sight of the unutterable passion of that look I could hardly contain myself. I was no longer satisfied with correcting crude poems. My whole being longed to express itself in some worthy action. At last I thought I would devote myself to making widow-remarriage popular in my country. I was prepared not only to speak and write on the subject, but also to spend money for the cause.

Nabin began to argue with me. "Permanent widowhood," said he, "has in it a sense of immense purity and peace, a calm beauty like that of the silent places of the dead shimmering in the wan light of the eleventh moon. Would not the mere possibility of remarriage destroy its divine beauty?"

Now this sort of sentimentality always makes me furious. In time of famine, if a well-fed man speaks scornfully of food, and advises a starving man at point of death to glut his hunger on the fragrance of flowers and the song of birds, what are we to think of him? I said with some heat, "Look here, Nabin, to the artist a ruin may be a beautiful object, but houses are built not only for the contemplation of artists, but that people may live therein, so they have to be kept in repair in spite of artistic susceptibilities. It is all very well for you to idealise widowhood from your safe distance, but you should remember that within widowhood there is a sensitive human heart, throbbing with pain and desire."

I had an impression that the conversion of Nabin would be a difficult matter, so perhaps I was more impassioned than I needed to be. I was somewhat surprised to find at the conclusion of my little speech that Nabin after a single thoughtful sigh completely agreed with me. The even more convincing peroration which I felt I might have delivered was not needed!

After about a week Nabin came to me, and said that if I would help him he was prepared to lead the way by marrying a widow himself.

I was overjoyed. I embraced him effusively and promised him any money that might be required for the purpose. Then Nabin told me his story.

I learned that Nabin's loved one was not an imaginary being. It appeared that Nabin, too, had for some time adored a widow from a distance, but had not spoken of his feelings to any living soul. Then the magazines in which Nabin's poems, or rather my poems, used to appear had reached the fair one's hands, and the poems had not been ineffective.

He said, he had no idea that the widow knew how to read. He used to post the magazine, without disclosing the sender's name, addressed to the widow's brother. It was only a sort of fancy of his, a concession to his hopeless passion. It was flinging garlands before a deity, it is not the worshipper's affair whether the god knows or not, whether he accepts or ignores the offering.

Nabin particularly wanted me to understand that he had no definite end in view when on diverse pretexts he sought and made the acquaintance of the widow's brother. Any near relation of a loved one needs to have a special interest for the lover.

Then followed a long story about how an illness of the brother at last brought them together. The presence of the poet himself led to much discussion of the poems, and the discussion was not necessarily restricted to the subject out of which it arose.

After his recent defeat in argument at my hands, Nabin had mustered up courage to propose the widow for marriage. At first he could not gain her consent. But when he had made full use of my eloquent words, supplemented by a tear or two of his own, the fair one capitulated unconditionally. Some money was now wanted by her guardian to make arrangements.

"Take it at once," said I.

"But," Nabin went on, "you know it will be some months before I can appease my father sufficiently for him to continue my allowance. How are we to live in the meantime?" I wrote out the necessary cheque without a word, and then I said, "Now tell me who she is. You need not look on me as a possible rival, for I swear I will not write poems to her, and even if I do I will not send them to her brother, but to you!"

"Don't be absurd," said Nabin, "I have not kept back her name because I feared your rivalry! The fact is, she was very much perturbed at taking this unusual step, and had asked me not to talk about the matter to my friends. But it no longer matters, now that everything has been satisfactorily settled. She lives at No. 19, the house next to yours."

If my heart had been an iron boiler it would have burst. "So she has no objection to remarriage?" I asked.

"Not at the present moment," replied Nabin with a smile.

"And was it the poems alone which wrought the magic change?"

"Well, my poems were not so bad, you know," said Nabin, "Were they?"

I swore mentally.

But at whom was I to swear? At him? At myself? At Providence? All the same, I swore.

13
Giribala

I

Giribala is overflowing with exuberance of youth that seems spilling over in spray all around her, in the folds of her soft dress, the turning of her neck, the motion of her hands, in the rhythm of her steps, now quick now languid, in her tinkling anklets and ringing laughter, in her voice and glances. She would often been seen, wrapt in a blue silk, walking on her terrace, in an impulse of unaccountable restlessness. Her limbs seem eager to dance to the time of an inner music unceasing and unheard. She takes pleasure in merely moving her body, causing ripples to break out in the flood of her young life. She would suddenly pluck a leaf from a plant in the flower-pot and throw it up in the sky, and her bangles would give a sudden tinkle, and the careless grace of her hand, like a bird freed from its cage, would fly unseen in the air. With her swift fingers she would brush away from her dress a mere nothing, standing on tiptoe she would peep over her terrace walls for no cause whatever, and then with a rapid motion turn round to go to another direction, swinging her bunch of keys tied to a corner of her garment. She would loosen her hair in an untimely caprice, sitting before her mirror to do it up again, and then in a fit of laziness would fling herself upon her bed, like a line of stray moonlight slipping through some opening of the leaves, idling in the shadow.

She has no children and having been married in a wealthy family, has very little work to do. Thus she seems to be daily accumulating her own self without expenditure, till the vessel is brimming over with the seething surplus. She has her husband, but not under her control. She has grown up from a girl into a woman, yet escaping, through familiarity, her husband's notice.

When she was newly married and her husband, Gopinath, was attending his college. Though they lived under the same roof, he would create occasions to send her letters on tinted paper perfumed with rosewater, and would even gloat upon some exaggerated grievances of imaginary neglect of love.

Just then his father died and he became the sole owner of his property. Like an unseasoned piece of timber, the immature youth of Gopinath attracted parasites which began to bore into his substance. From now his movements took the course that led him in a contrary direction from his wife.

There is a dangerous fascination to be leaders of men, to which many strong minds have succumbed. To be accepted as the leader of a small circle of sycophants, in his own parlour, has the same fearful attraction for a man who suffers from a scarcity of brains and character. Gopinath assumed the part of a hero among his friends and acquaintances, and tried daily to invent new wonders in all manner of extravagance. He won a reputation among his followers for his audacity of excesses, which goaded him not only to keep up his fame, but to surpass him at all costs.

Meanwhile, Giribala, in the seclusion of her lonely youth, felt like a queen who had her throne, but no subjects. She knew she had the power in her hand which could make the world of men her captive, only that world itself was wanting.

Giribala had a maidservant whose name was Sudha. She could sing, dance and improvise verses, and she freely gives expression to her regret that such a beauty as that of her mistress should be dedicated to a fool who forgets to enjoy what he owns. Giribala is never tired of hearing from her the details of her charms, while at the same time contradicting her, calling her a liar and a flatterer, exciting her to swear by all that is sacred that she is earnest in her admiration, which statement, even without the accompaniment of a solemn oath, is not difficult for Giribala to believe.

Sudha used to sing to her a song beginning with the line, "Let me write myself a slave upon the soles of thy feet," and Giribala in her imagination could feel that her beautiful feet were fully worthy of bearing inscriptions of everlasting slavery from conquered hearts, if only they could be free in their career of conquest.

But the woman to whom her husband Gopinath has surrendered himself as a slave is Lavanga, the actress. She had the reputation of playing to perfection the part of a maiden languishing in hopeless love and swooning on the stage with an exquisite naturalness. When her husband had not altogether vanished from her sphere of influence, Giribala had often heard from him about the wonderful histrionic powers of this woman and in her jealous curiosity had greatly desired to see Lavanga on the stage. But she could not secure her husband's consent, because Gopinath was firm in his opinion that the theatre was a place not fit for any decent woman to visit.

At last, she paid for a seat and sent Sudha to see this famous actress in one of her best parts. The account that she received from her on her return was far from flattering to Lavanga, both as to her personal appearance and her stage accomplishments. As, for obvious reasons, she had great faith in Sudha's power of appreciation, where it was due, Giribala did not hesitate to believe her in her description of Lavanga, which was accompanied by a mimicry of a ludicrous mannerism.

When at last her husband deserted her in his infatuation for this woman, she began to feel qualms of doubt. But as Sudha repeatedly asserted her former opinion with ever greater vehemence, comparing Lavanga to a piece of burnt log dressed up in a woman's clothes, Giribala determined secretly to go to the theatre herself and settle this question for good.

One night, she went to the theatre with all the excitement of a forbidden entry. Her very trepidation of heart lent a special charm to what she saw. She gazed at the faces of the spectators, lit up with an unnatural shine of lamplight and with the magic of its music and the painted canvas of its scenery, the theatre seemed to her like a world where society was suddenly freed from its law of gravitation.

Coining from her walled up terrace and joyless home, she had entered a region where dreams and reality had clasped their hands in friendship, over the wine cup of art.

The bell rang, the orchestra music stopped, the audience sat still in their seats, the stagelights shone brighter, and the curtain was drawn up. Suddenly appeared in the light, from the mystery of the unseen, the shepherd girls of the Vrinda forest, and with the accompaniment of songs commenced their dance, punctuated with the uproarious applause of the audience. The blood began to throb all over Giribala's body, and she forgot for the moment that her life was limited to the circumstances and that she was not free in a world where all laws had melted in music.

Sudha came occasionally to interrupt her with her anxious whispers urging her to hasten back home for the fear of being detected. But she paid no heed to her warning, for her sense of fear had gone.

The play goes on. Krishna has given offence to his beloved Radha and she in her wounded pride refuses to recognize him. He is entreating her, abasing himself at her feet, but in vain. Giribala's heart seems to swell. She imagines herself as offended Radha, and feels that she also has in her this woman's power to vindicate her pride. She had heard what a force was woman's beauty in the world but to-night it became to her palpable.

At last the curtain dropped, the light grew dim, the audience got ready to leave the theatre, but Giribala sat still like one in a dream. The thought that she would have to go home had vanished from her mind. She waited for the curtain to rise again and the eternal theme of Krishna's humiliation at the feet of Radha to continue. But Sudha came to remind her that the play had ended and the lamps would soon be put out.

It was late when Giribala came back home. A kerosene lamp was dimly burning in the melancholy solitude and silence of her room. Near the window upon her lonely bed a mosquito curtain was gently moving in the breeze. Her world seemed to her distasteful and mean like a rotten fruit swept into the dustbin.

From that day, she regularly visited the theatre every Saturday. The fascination of her first sight of it lost much of its glamour. The painted vulgarity of the actresses and the falseness of their affectations became more and more evident, yet the habit grew upon her. Every time the curtain rose, the window of her life's prison-house seemed to open before her and the stage, bordered off from the world of reality by its gilded frame and scenic display, by its array of lights and even its flimsiness of conventionalism, appeared to her like a fairyland where it was not impossible for herself to occupy the throne of the fairy queen.

When for the first time she saw her husband among the audience shouting his drunken admiration for a certain actress she felt an intense disgust and prayed in her mind that a day might come when she might have an opportunity to spurn him away with her contempt. But the opportunity became rarer every day, for Gopinath was hardly ever to be seen at his home now, being carried away, one knew not where, in the centre of a duststorm of dissipation.

One evening in the month of March, in the light of the full moon, Giribala was sitting on her terrace dressed in her cream-coloured robe. It was her habit daily to deck herself with jewellery as if for some festive occasion. For these costly gems were like wine to her, they sent heightened consciousness of beauty to her limbs, she felt like a plant in spring tingling with the impulse of flowers in all its branches. She wore a pair of diamond bracelets on her arms, a necklace of rubies and pearls on her neck, and a ring with a big sapphire on the little finger of her left hand. Sudha was sitting near her bare feet admiringly touching them with her hand and expressing her wish that she were a man privileged to offer her life as homage to such a pair of feet.

Sudha gently hummed a lovesong to her and the evening wore on to night. Everybody in the household had finished their evening meal, and had gone to sleep. When suddenly Gopinath appeared reeking with scent and liquor, and Sudha drawing for cloth-end over her face, hastily ran away from the terrace.

Giribala thought for a moment that her day had come at last. She turned away her face and sat silent.

But the curtain in her stage did not rise and no song of entreaty came from her hero, with the words, "Listen to the pleading of the moonlight, my love, and hide not thy face."

In his dry unmusical voice Gopinath said, "Give me your keys."

A gust of south wind like a sigh of the insulted romance of the poetic world scattered all over the terrace the smell of the night-blooming jasmines and loosened some wisp of hair on Giribala's cheek. She let go her pride, and got up and said, "You shall have your keys if you listen to what I have to say." Gopinath said, "I cannot delay. Give me your keys."

Giribala said, "I will give you the keys and everything that is in the safe, but you must not leave me."

Gopinath said, "That cannot be. I have urgent business."

"Then you shan't have the keys," said Giribala.

Gopinath began to search for them. He opened the drawers of the dressing table, broke open the lid of the box that contained Giribala's toilet requisites, smashed the glass panes of her almirah, groped under the pillows and mattress of the bed, but the keys he could not find. Giribala stood near the door stiff and silent like a marble image gazing at vacancy. Trembling with rage, Gopinath came to her and said with an angry growl, "Give me your keys or you will repent." Giribala did not answer and Gopinath, pinning her to the wall, snatched away by force her bracelets, necklace and ring, gave her a parting kick and went away.

Nobody in the house woke up from his sleep, none in the neighbourhood knew of this outrage, the moonlight remained placid and the peace of the night undisturbed. Hearts can be rent never to heal again amidst such serene silence.

Next morning, Giribala said she was going to see her father and left home. As Gopinath's present destination was not known and she was not responsible to anybody else in the house her absence was not noticed.

II

The new play of 'Manorama' was on rehearsal in the theatre where Gopinath was a constant visitor. Lavanga was practising for the part of the heroine Manorama, and Gopinath, sitting in the front seat with his rabble of followers, would vociferously encourage his favourite actress with his approbation. This greatly disturbed the rehearsal but the proprietors of the theatre did not dare to annoy their patron of whose vindictiveness they were afraid. But one day he went so far as to molest an actress in the Greenroom and he had to be turned away by the aid of the police.

Gopinath determined to take his revenge, and when, after a great deal of preparation and shrieking advertisements, the new play 'Manorama' was about to be produced, Gopinath took away the principal actress Lavanga with him and disappeared. It was a great shock to the manager, who had to postpone the opening night, and, getting hold of a new actress, taught her the part, and brought out the play before the public with considerable misgivings in his mind.

But the success was as unexpected as it was unprecedented. When its news reached Gopinath he could not resist his curiosity to come and see the performance.

The play opens with Manorama living in her husband's house neglected and hardly noticed. Near the end of the drama her husband deserts her and concealing his first marriage manages to marry a millionaire's daughter. When the wedding ceremony is over and the bridal veil is raised from her face she is discovered to be the same Manorama, only no longer the former drudge, but queenly in her beauty and splendour of dress and ornaments. In her infancy she had been brought up in a poor home being kidnapped from the house of her rich father, who having traced her to her husband's home, has brought her back to him and celebrates her marriage once again in a fitting manner.

In the concluding scene, when the husband is going through his period of penitence and humiliation, as is fit in a play which has its moral, a sudden disturbance arose among the audience. So long as Manorama appeared obscured in her position of drudgery, Gopinath showed no sign of perturbation.

But when after the wedding ceremony, she came out dressed in her red bridal robe and took her veil off, when with a majestic pride of her overwhelming beauty she turned her face towards the audience and, slightly bending he neck, shot a fiery glance of exultation at Gopinath, applause broke out in wave after wave and the enthusiasm of the spectators became unbounded.

Suddenly Gopinath cried out, "Giribala!" and rushed like a madman upon the stage. The audience shouted and the police came to drag him away. He struggled and screamed, "I will kill her," while the curtain dropped.

14
The Parrot's Training

Once upon a time there was a bird. It was ignorant. The bird sang well, but couldn't recite scriptures. It hopped pretty frequently, but lacked manners.

The Raja said to himself, "Ignorance is costly in the long run, for fools consume as much food as their betters and yet give nothing in return."

He called his nephews to his presence and told them that the bird must have a sound schooling.

The pundits were summoned. They at once went to the root of the matter.

They said that the ignorance of birds was due to their natural habit of living in poor nests. Therefore, according to the pundits, the first thing necessary for this bird's education was a suitable cage.

The pundits had their rewards and went back home happily.

A golden cage was built with gorgeous decorations. Crowds came to see it from all parts of the world. "Culture, captured and caged!" exclaimed some, in a rapture of ecstasy, and burst into tears. Others remarked, "Even if culture be missed, the cage will remain, to the end, a substantial fact. How fortunate for the bird!"

The goldsmith filled his bag with money and lost no time in sailing homewards.

The pundit sat down to educate the bird. With proper deliberation he took his pinch of snuff, as he said, "Textbooks can never be too many for our purpose!"

The nephews brought together an enormous crowd of scribes. They copied from books, and copied from copies, till the manuscripts were piled up to an unreachable height. Men murmured in amazement, "Oh, the tower of culture, egregiously high! The end of it lost in the clouds!"

The scribes with light hearts, hurried home, their pockets heavily laden.

The nephews were furiously busy keeping the cage in proper trim. As their constant scrubbing and polishing went on, the people said with satisfaction, "This is progress indeed!"

Men were employed in large numbers, and supervisors were still more numerous. These, with their cousins of all different degrees of distance, built a palace for themselves and lived there happily ever after.

Whatever may be its other deficiencies, the world is never in want of 'fault-finders' and they went about saying that every creature remotely connected with the cage flourished beyond words, excepting only the bird.

When this remark reached the Raja's ears, he summoned his nephews before him and said, "My dear nephews, what is this that we hear?"

The nephews said in answer, "Sire, let the testimony of the goldsmiths and the pundits, the scribes and the supervisors, be taken, if the truth is to be known. Food is scarce with the fault-finders, and that is why their tongues have gained in sharpness."

The explanation was so luminously satisfactory that the Raja decorated each one of his nephews with his own rare jewels.

The Raja at length, being desirous of seeing with his own eyes how his Department of Education busied itself with the little bird, made his appearance one day at the Great Hall of Learning.

From the gate rose the sounds of conch-shells and gongs, horns, bugles and trumpets, cymbals, drums and kettle-drums, tomtoms, tambourines, flutes, fifes, barrel-organs and bagpipes. The pundits began chanting mantras with their topmost voices, while the goldsmiths, scribes, supervisors, and their numberless cousins of all different degrees of distance, loudly raised a round of cheers.

The nephews smiled and said, "Sire, what do you think of it all?"

The Raja said, "It does seem so fearfully like a sound principle of education!"

Mightily pleased, the Raja was about to remount his elephant, when the fault-finder, from behind some bush, cried out, "Maharaja, have you seen the bird?"

"Indeed, I have not!" exclaimed the Raja, "I completely forgot about the bird."

Turning back, he asked the pundits about the method they followed in instructing the bird. It was shown to him. He was immensely impressed. The method was so stupendous that the bird looked ridiculously unimportant in comparison. The Raja was satisfied that there was no flaw in the arrangements. As for any complaint from the bird itself, that simply could not be expected. Its throat was so completely choked with the leaves from the books that it could neither whistle nor whisper. It sent a thrill through one's body to watch the process.

This time, while remounting his elephant, the Raja ordered his state ear-puller to give a thorough good pull at both the ears of the fault-finder.

The bird thus crawled on, duly and properly, to the safest verge of inanity. In fact, its progress was satisfactory in the extreme. Nevertheless, nature occasionally triumphed over training, and when the morning light peeped into the bird's cage it sometimes fluttered its wings in a reprehensible manner. And, though it is hard to believe, it pitifully pecked at its bars with its feeble beak.

"What impertinence!" growled the kotwal.

The blacksmith, with his forge and hammer, took his place in the Raja's Department of Education. Oh, what resounding blows! The iron chain was soon completed, and the bird's wings were clipped.

The Raja's brothers-in-law looked black, and shook their heads, saying, "These birds not only lack good sense, but also gratitude!"

With textbook in one hand and baton in the other, the pundits gave the poor bird what may fitly be called lessons!

The kotwal was honoured with a title for his watchfulness, and the blacksmith for his skill in forging chains.

The bird died.

Nobody had the least notion how long ago this had happened. The fault-finder was the first man to spread the rumour.

The Raja called his nephews and asked them. "My dear nephews, what is this that we hear?"

The nephews said, "Sire, the bird's education has been completed."

"Does it hop?" the Raja enquired.

"Never!" said the nephews.

"Does it fly?"

"No."

"Bring me the bird," said the Raja.

The bird was brought to him, guarded by the kotwal and the sepoys and the sowars. The Raja poked its body with his finger. Only its inner stuffing of book-leaves rustled.

Outside the window, the murmur of the spring breeze amongst the newly budded asoka leaves made the April morning wistful.

15
The Renunciation

I

It was a full moon night, early in the month of Phalgun. The youthful spring was everywhere sending forth its breeze laden with the fragrance of mango-blossoms. The melodious notes of an untiring papiya, who was known by the Anglo-Indian writers as 'brain-fever bird', which is a sheer libel, concealed within the thick foliage of an old litchi tree by the side of a tank, penetrated a sleepless bedroom of the Mukerji family. There Hemanta now restlessly twisted a lock of his wife's hair round his finger, now beat her churl against her wristlet until it tinkled, now pulled at the chaplet of flowers about her head, and left it hanging over her face. His mood was that of as evening breeze which played about a favourite flowering shrub, gently shaking her now this side, now that, in the hope of rousing her to animation.

But Kusum sat motionless, looking out of the open window, with eyes immersed in the moonlit depth of never-ending space beyond. Her husband's caresses were lost on her.

At last Hemanta clasped both the hands of his wife, and shaking them gently and said, "Kusum, where are you? You seem to have receded so far away. See how beautiful the night is."

Kusum turned her eyes from the void of space towards her husband, and said slowly, "I know a mantra which could in one moment shatter this spring night and the moon into pieces."

"If you do," laughed Hemanta, "pray don't utter it. If any mantra of yours could bring three or four Saturdays during the week, and prolong the nights till 5 p.m. the next day, say it by all means."

Saying this, he tried to draw his wife a little closer to him. Kusum, freeing herself from the embrace, said, "Do you know, tonight I feel a longing to tell you what I promised to reveal only on my death-bed. Tonight I feel that I could endure whatever punishment you might inflict on me."

Hemanta was on the point of making a jest about punishments by reciting a verse from Jayadeva, when the sound of an angry pair of slippers was heard approaching rapidly. They were the familiar footsteps of his father, Haribar Mukerji, and Hemanta, not knowing what it meant, was in a flutter of excitement.

Standing outside the door Harihar roared out, "Hemanta, turn your wife out of the house immediately."

Hemanta looked at his wife, and detected no trace of surprise in her features. She merely buried her face within the palms of her hands, and, with all the strength and intensity of her soul, wished that she could then and there melt into nothingness. It was the same papiya whose song floated into the room with the south breeze, and no one heard it. Endless are the beauties of the earth-but alas, how easily everything is twisted out of shape.

II

Returning from without, Hemanta asked his wife, "Is it true?"

"It is," replied Kusum.

"Why didn't you tell me long ago?"

"I did try many a time, and I always failed. I am a wretched woman."

"Then tell me everything now."

Kusum gravely told her story in a firm unshaken voice. She waded barefooted through fire, as it were, with slow unflinching steps, and nobody knew how much she was scorched. Having heard her to the end, Hemanta rose and walked out.

Kusum thought that her husband had gone, never to return again. It did not strike her as strange. She took it as naturally as any other incident of everyday life, so dry and apathetic had her mind become during the last few moments. Only the world and love seemed to her as a void and make-believe from beginning to end. Even the memory of the protestations of love, which her husband had made to her in days past, brought to her lips a dry, hard, joyless smile, like a sharp cruel knife which had cut through her heart. She was thinking, perhaps, that the love which seemed to fill so much of one's life, which brought in its train such fondness and depth of feeling, which made even the briefest separation so exquisitely painful and a moment's union so intensely sweet, which seemed boundless in its extent and eternal in its duration, the cessation of which could not be imagined even in births to come, this was that love! So feeble was its support! No sooner does the priesthood touch it than your 'eternal' love crumbles into a handful of dust! Only a short while ago Hemanta had whispered to her, "What a beautiful night!" The same night was not yet at an end, the same papiya was still warbling, the same south breeze still blew into the roam, making the bed-curtain shiver, the same moonlight lay on the bed next the open window, sleeping like a beautiful heroine exhausted with gaiety. All this was unreal! Love was more falsely dissembling than she herself!

III

The next morning Hemanta, fagged after a sleepless night, and looking like one distracted, called at the house of Peari Sankar Ghosal. "What news, my son?" Peari Sankar greeted him.

Hemanta, flaring up like a big fire, said in a trembling voice, "You have defiled our caste. You have brought destruction upon us. And you will have to pay for it." He could say no more, he felt choked.

"And you have preserved my caste, presented my ostracism from the community, and patted me on the back affectionately!" said Peari Sankar with a slight sarcastic smile.

Hemanta wished that his Brahmin-fury could reduce Peari Sankar to ashes in a moment, but his rage burnt only himself. Peari Sankar sat before him unscathed, and in the best of health.

"Did I ever do you any harm?" demanded Hemanta in a broken voice.

"Let me ask you one question," said Peari Sankar.

"My daughter, my only child, what harm had she done your father? You were very young then, and probably never heard. Listen, then. Now, don't you excite yourself. There is much humour in what I am going to relate.

"You were quite small when my son-in-law Nabakanta ran away to England after stealing my daughter's jewels. You might truly remember the commotion in the village when he returned as a barrister five years later. Or, perhaps, you were unaware of it, as you were at school in Calcutta at the time. Your father, arrogating to himself the headship of the community, declared that if I sent my daughter to her husband's home, I must renounce her for good, and never again allow her to cross my threshold. I fell at your father's feet, and implored him, saying, "Brother, save me once! I will make the boy swallow cow-dung, and go through the *prayaschittam* ceremony. Do take him back into caste." But your father remained obdurate. For my part, I could not disown my only child, and, bidding good-bye to my village and my kinsmen, I betook myself to Calcutta. There, too, my troubles followed me. When I had made every arrangement for my nephew's marriage, your father stirred up the girl's people, and they broke the match off. Then I took a solemn vow that, if there was a drop of Brahmin blood flowing in my veins, I would avenge myself. You understand the business to some extent now, don't you?

But wait a little longer. You will enjoy it, when I tell you the whole story, it is interesting.

"When you were attending college, one Bipradas Chatterji used to live next door to your lodgings. The poor fellow is dead now. In his house lived a child-widow called Kusum, the destitute orphan of a Kayestha gentleman. The girl was very pretty, and the old Brahmin desired to shield her from the hungry gaze of college students. But for a young girl to throw dust in the eyes of her old guardian was not at all a difficult task. She often went to the top of the roof, to hang her washing out to dry, and, I believe, you found your own roof best suited for your studies. Whether you two spoke to each other, when on your respective roofs, I cannot tell, but the girl's behaviour excited suspicion in the old man's mind. She made frequent mistakes in her household duties, and, like Parbati (The wife of Shiva the Destroyer), engaged in her devotions, began gradually to renounce food and sleep. Some evenings she would burst into tears in the presence of the old gentleman, without any apparent reason.

"At last he discovered that you two saw each other from the roofs pretty frequently, and that you even went the length of absenting yourself from college to sit on the roof at mid-day with a book in your hand, so fond had you grown suddenly of solitary study. Bipradas came to me for advice, and told me everything. "Uncle," said I to him, "for a long while you have cherished a desire to go on a pilgrimage to Benares. You had better do it now, and leave the girl in my charge. I will take care of her."

"So he went. I lodged the girl in the house of Sripati Chatterji, passing him off as her father. What happened next is known to you. I feel a great relief today, having told you everything from the beginning. It sounds like a romance, doesn't it? I think of turning it into a book, and getting it printed. But I am not a writing-man myself. They say my nephew has some aptitude that way. I will get him to write it for me. But the best thing would be, if you would collaborate with him, because the conclusion of the story is not known to me so well."

Without paying much attention to the concluding remarks of Peari Sankar, Hemanta asked, "Did not Kusum object to this marriage?"

"Well," said Peari Sankar, "it is very difficult to guess." You know, my boy, how women's minds are constituted. When they say "no" they mean "yes." During the first few days after she had gone to her new home, she went almost crazy at not seeing you. You, too, seemed to have discovered her new address somehow, as you used to lose your way after starting for college, and loiter about in front of Sripati's house. Your eyes did not appear to be exactly in search of the Presidency College, as they were directed towards the barred windows of a private house, through which nothing but insects and the hearts of moon-struck young men could obtain access. I felt very sorry for you both. I could see that your studies were being seriously interrupted, and that the plight of the girl was pitiable also.

One day, I called Kusum to me and said, "Listen to me, my daughter. I am an old man, and you need feel no delicacy in my presence. I know whom you desire at heart. The young man's condition is hopeless too. I wish I could bring about your union." At this Kusum suddenly melted into tears, and ran away. On several evenings after that, I visited Sripati's house, and, calling Kusum to me, discussed with her matters relating to you, and so I succeeded in gradually overcoming her shyness. At last, when I said that I would try to bring about a marriage, she asked me, "How can it be?"

"Never mind," I said, "I would pass you off as a Brahmin maiden." After a good deal of argument, she begged me to find out whether you would approve of it. "What nonsense!" replied I, "The boy is well-nigh mad as it were, what's the use of disclosing all these complications to him? Let the ceremony be over smoothly and then-all's well that ends well. Especially, as there is not the slightest risk of its ever leaking out, why go out of the way to make a fellow miserable for life?"

"I do not know whether the plan had Kusum's assent or not. At times she wept, and at other times she remained silent. If I said, "Let us drop it then," she would become very restless. When things were in this state, I sent Sripati to you with the proposal of marriage, you consented without a moment's hesitation. Everything was settled."

"Shortly before the day fixed, Kusum became so obstinate that I had the greatest difficulty in bringing her round again. "Do let it drop, uncle," she said to me constantly. "What do you mean, you silly child," I rebuked her, "how can we back out now, when everything has been settled?"

"Spread a rumour that I am dead," she implored, "Send me away somewhere."

"What would happen to the young man then?" said I. "He is now in the seventh heaven of delight, expecting that his long cherished desire would be fulfilled to-morrow, and today you want me to send him the news of your death. The result would be that to-morrow I should have to bear the news of his death to you, and the same evening your death would be reported to me. Do you imagine, child, that I am capable of committing a girl-murder and a Brahmin-murder at my age?"

"Eventually the happy marriage was celebrated at the auspicious moment, and I felt relieved of a burdensome duty which I owed to myself. What happened afterwards you know best."

"Couldn't you stop after having done us an irreparable injury?" burst out Hemanta after a short silence. "Why have you told the secret now?"

With the utmost composure, Peari Sankar replied, "When I saw that all arrangements had been made for the wedding of your sister, I said to myself, "Well, I have fouled the caste of one Brahmin, but that was only from a sense of duty. Here, another Brahmin's caste is imperilled, and this time it is my plain duty to prevent it." So I wrote to them saying that I was in a position to prove that you had taken the daughter of a *sudra* to wife."

Controlling himself with a gigantic effort, Hemanta said, "What will become of this girl whom I shall abandon now? Would you give her food and shelter?"

"I have done what was mine to do," replied Peari Sankar calmly. "It is no part of my duty to look after the discarded wives of other people. Anybody there? Get a glass of coconut milk for Hemanta Babu with ice in it. And some pan too."

Hemanta rose, and took his departure without waiting for this luxurious hospitality.

IV

It was the fifth night of the waning of the moon and the night was dark. No birds were singing. The lichi tree by the tank looked like a smudge of ink on a background a shade less deep. The south wind was blindly roaming about in the darkness like a sleep-walker. The stars in the sky with vigilant unblinking eyes were trying to penetrate the darkness, in their effort to fathom some profound mystery.

No light shone in the bedroom. Hemanta was sitting on the side of the bed next the open window, gazing at the darkness in front of him. Kusum lay on the floor, clasping her husband's feet with both her arms, and her face resting on them. Time stood like an ocean hushed into stillness. On the background of eternal night, fate seemed to have painted this one single picture for all time—annihilation on every side, the judge in the centre of it, and the guilty one at his feet.

The sound of slippers was heard again. Approaching the door, Harihar Mukerji said, "You have had enough time, I can't allow you more. Turn the girl out of the house."

Kusum, as she heard this, embraced her husband's feet with all the ardour of a lifetime, covered them with kisses, and touching her forehead to them reverentially, withdrew herself.

Hemanta rose, and walking to the door and said, "Father, I won't forsake my wife."

"What!" roared out Harihar, "Would you lose your caste, then?"

"I don't care," Hemanta calmly replied.

"Then I renounce you too."